W9-BFM-047

The Third Life of Per Smevik

The Third Life of Per Smevik

By

O. E. Rølvaag

Translated by

Ella Valborg Tweet and Solveig Zempel

Dillon Press, Inc. Minneapolis

Dillon Press, Inc.
Minneapolis, Minnesota 55401

International Standard Book Number: 0-87518-045-0
Library of Congress Catalog Card Number: 71-172872

Printed in the United States of America

Table of Contents

Introduction

Ole Edvart Rølvaag was born on April 22, 1876, on the island of Dønna, which lies just below the Arctic Circle. He was the third child, and the second son in a family of eight children born to Peder Benjamin and Ellerine (Ella) Jakobsen Rølvaag. The family had lived for six generations on this rocky cove at Rølvaag, on the barren, windswept spit of land jutting out into the sea—so windswept that no trees grew there. It was just rock and peatlands, brush and heather—and the sea rolling in. Here they were all fishermen, who maintained small fields in the clefts—growing barley and rye, potatoes and a few root crops, grazing a few cattle on the home pastures, and a few sheep on the nearest islands.

Before the children were old enough to walk, they crawled down the rocky path to the sea, and on calm days they could lie in a boat and peer down into the mysteries of the bottom, or they could improvise a line and fish, or watch the flocks of eider ducks, or the noisy, swooping gulls. In summer, the ever-present daylight, the golden, shimmering light when the sun rolled toward the horizon, but never quite disappeared, the purple heather, the wild daisies, the violas, and the bluebells created a fairyland atmosphere. In winter, the darkness, the storms, the loneliness when the men were away with the fishing fleet, and above all the wind and the pounding sea caused both young and old to feel as if judgment day were at hand. Small wonder that sensitive souls were either wildly happy or deeply depressed!

The home at the hamlet of Rølvaag was a modest one—

beyond the low door (one had both to step high and stoop low to avoid falling into the hall) were two large rooms. Behind the kitchen was a larder, at one end of the living room was a narrow little bedroom; up above, under the sod roof was a low-ceilinged sleeping loft. This house, as well as others at Rølvaag faced across the cove. Opposite, on the southern end of the island lay a mountain which resembled a sleeping giant.

The atmosphere of the home was warm and affectionate. The father, Peder Benjamin Jakobsen, was a skilled carpenter as well as a good fisherman. Although he had little schooling, he was known as an intelligent man—pious, strong-willed to the point of obstinacy, and argumentative. It is told of him that when the pastor came to the nearest church on his monthly visits to the parish, Peder Benjamin would trudge the seven miles to Dønnes to debate some obscure Biblical point. Mother Ella has been described as an unusually fine person, quiet, calm, understanding, and there seems to have developed a very close relationship between her and the young Ole.

From his own accounts, Ole had a happy childhood—like all the other children of the family, he had to perform simple tasks: watching out for the younger children, helping his mother gather seaweed which she cooked to feed the cattle, occasionally herding the cattle or sheep, helping to turn the blocks of peat which had been set up in the sun to dry for fuel, and learning to mend the nets and take care of the fishing gear. The boys even learned to knit, for the mother made almost all the clothing for the family, spinning the wool from their own sheep, knitting socks and mittens, and weaving homespun for both inner and outer clothing. But in spite of the chores and the poverty, childhood was a happy time.

When he was about six, however, and was to learn to

read, it was another story. The oldest brother, Johan, was quick and learned rapidly; sister Martha hung over the table watching Johan, and she seemed to learn almost as fast as he—learning to read the alphabet upside down. But for Ole, it was pure torture. He told it himself: "Father was a voracious reader and read well aloud; Mother also was fond of reading, though she never found much time for it. Then I came along! No, I didn't come at all. I was the black sheep. I am not overstating the case, I'm simply telling how it was. Had it not been for Mother and my sister, I'd most likely have been given up as hopeless. When Father tried to teach me, he soon lost patience and boxed my ears, which made me cry; the crying only blurred my sight, making reading impossible. It went better with my brother as teacher, for him I could sauce; then there'd be a fight and the torture would end . . .

"Soon, the name *tyrk* (meaning literally a Turk) was applied to me. I was the incarnation of an illiterate Turk. In time I'd have to be sent to Turkey, which prospect didn't bother me so much—just let me break away once! . . ."

From the age of seven, until confirmation at the age of fourteen, the children trudged more than seven miles to school. The school year was only nine weeks, divided into three terms of three weeks each, one term coming in midwinter, one in the spring, and one in the early fall. During the spring and fall, the Rølvaag children walked to and from school each day, making a round trip of almost fifteen miles. There were no roads at that time, only footpaths across the moorlands and swamps and an occasional meadow. During the winter term they stayed at a farm near the school, where they were housed in dormitory-like rooms, the boys on one side of the hall, the girls on the other. In the evenings, after lessons had been studied, there was much lively play, but even more of storytelling.

The children carried their own provisions. The fare was very simple—sour milk, a little butter and bread. No cheeses or jellies, and no cooked food. On Saturdays they went home for a new supply, leaving for school again early Monday morning.

When, at the age of seven, Ole started school, his reading ability improved, and soon he could read with the best of them. But he always felt overshadowed by his beloved older brother, and he finished school at fourteen, feeling inadequate and not worth further education.

Though the instruction was largely religious, pupils with initiative might gather a variety of information, for the teacher was talented and well-educated. Norway at this time was in the midst of a remarkable era of enlightenment; book collections and book clubs were found everywhere. Libraries were established at the fishing stations, and the community where the school was located also had a parish library. The boys from Rølvaag were among the most avid of the readers. Each week they made trips to borrow, not one, but five or six books. The library was housed at the home of one of their schoolmates, who recalled how he and the two boys from Rølvaag would sit upstairs in the loft and discuss what they had been reading. When they had almost exhausted the resources of the library, they sat one day and debated how they could get new books to read. Young Ole finally piped up, "Perhaps we could write to King Oscar?" They all burst out laughing at the preposterousness of the whole idea, Ole loudest of all. But one of the boys did write, and though they did not get a reply from the King himself, they did receive a letter from a government official, promising them new books. And when word reached Rølvaag that the addition to the library had finally arrived, the boys lost no time in trotting the seven miles to examine their treasure!

The library had books to suit many tastes—from fiction, both dime novels and the classics, to history, geography and geology. The boys read poetry, drama and novels. The first novel that Ole remembered reading was a good Norwegian translation of Cooper's *The Last of the Mohicans*. And it was this novel, he admitted later, which first sparked his interest in America. In addition to the books which the children brought home from the library, the family subscribed to a newspaper from Oslo, and from all accounts, the paper was read thoroughly and both foreign and domestic questions were debated. In spite of poverty and the distance from the great centers, the family was remarkably well-read and informed.

With confirmation, schooling was ended for Ole. The following January, 1891, as a fourteen-year-old, he sailed north to the Lofoten fishing banks. The winters of 1892 and 1893, when he was still considered a novice, he counted for only "half a man" in the profit-sharing crew. Though he has been described as slight of build, and not particularly strong, he had both willpower and pride that would not let him be outdone, characteristics which stayed with him through his entire life and which no doubt affected his health in later years.

During the winter of 1893 the fishermen at Lofoten experienced the worst storm ever recorded. On the twenty-fifth of January the entire fleet lay out on the banks, and the sea was boiling with fish, so though the skies warned of bad weather, the men paid no attention. Suddenly the storm broke—Ole described it later: "I've seen storms strike suddenly before this and later as well, but never with the suddenness of this one—it was as if it had been let out of a sack! Although three men—strong men all—sat at the oars keeping the boat steady, the first fierce gust of wind threw her sideways as if she had been a matchstick. And then came a blinding blizzard and darkness." Only the seamanship of the leader of the crew—Kristian Andersen—and the sheer willpower of the men in the boat brought them through the storm. Hardest of all, Rølvaag later said, was to hear crew after crew, most of them friends, go down around them, and not be able to give them a hand. They finally reached land, more dead than alive, bleeding at the mouth and nose. Although he was to stay with the fishing fleet through the next three winters, and fish in the home waters each summer, it was no doubt this storm experience that first led him to consider leaving home and to seek something better to do with his life.

Friends from this period of his life have described him as the central figure of the group, very lively, full of fun and jokes, with a sweetheart in every hamlet. He was known as a good fisherman and an excellent seaman, self-reliant, and with more than the usual endowment of determination. In spite of the lively side of his nature, he was deeply serious as well. And more and more he felt an intense longing for something better, felt that greater opportunities and greater challenges were waiting for him somewhere.

Following the dreadful storm of 1893 he wrote to his uncle who had emigrated to South Dakota, and asked him to lend the money for a ticket to America. The answer was long in coming. He was to spend three more seasons at Lofoten. But in June, 1896, he received a ticket which would bring him to Elk Point, South Dakota late that summer.

Yet the decision to leave home was a difficult one to make. He was deeply attached to his family, especially his mother; the sea and the home on the island had strong ties for him. But just at the time he had made up his mind to leave Norway a tempting opportunity was offered, and he had to review his decision whether to leave or to stay.

Every year a fair was held at Bjørn, one of the small villages on the east coast of the island of Dønna. On the first Tuesday, Wednesday and Thursday of July each year, that village was swarming with people. Tradesmen from as far away as Bergen to the south, and the towns in Finnmark to the north, came to show their wares. Booths and tents were set up, and hawkers of every description called to the passers-by. Clowns and magicians, dance hall proprietors and lay preachers tried to catch the attention of young and old; music from the ferris wheels and carrousels added to the din. Officers in bright uniforms, and government officials with their badges and sashes stood out in the crowd. And one of the bright spots for some of the young people were the book dealers who set up shop and did good business on these days.

The twenty-year-old Ole Pedersen Rølvaag was among those who attended the market at Bjørn in July of 1896. He had rowed over with his old friend and skipper, Kristian Andersen. On the way over, Ole had finally confessed that he was going to leave Norway and go to America. Kristian answered quickly that he should forget such nonsense. When they came ashore, they walked along the beach where the Nordland boats were displayed. They stopped before one particularly beautiful one, admired the sleek lines, the especially good proportions. As they stood there together, Kristian Andersen ran his hand along the upturned keel, then turned and looked sharply at Ole: "You know that I'm not a poor man now. If you will stay, and give up this notion of going to America, I'll buy this boat for you, and make you the skipper. If the fishing is good this winter, you'll have her paid for in a year."

The young man begged for time to think this over, and left the noisy fair. He climbed to a height above the noise and the racket, away from the merrymaking and the dancing.

"It was a fine, clear day in Nordland," he recalled later. "I could see a long way across the water. I sat there gazing off across the fjord trying to make out the unsubstantial shapes of my dreams and aspirations. What ought I to do? How could I refuse such a splendid offer? . . . . I had to decide something. Life had made me tragic. Would my heart stop aching as I set sail, as I paid for the boat and grew prosperous as the years went by? . . . On the other hand, what was my heart aching for? I honestly didn't know. If I decided to refuse this wonderful offer, what reasonable excuse could I make? You see, I *had* no valid excuse, or none that could be put into words. I just felt that I wasn't fulfilling myself. I wanted to go away, find out what the world was like, and see if I didn't fit in somewhere else. But how can you explain that to sensible, practical people? To their minds, you're simply acting like a headstrong fool."

But when he came down the mountainside that afternoon, he told his friend Kristian Andersen that he was leaving for South Dakota.

According to a diary which he kept sporadically for the next few years, he left home soon after. The ocean voyage was a pleasure; as he reported in his letters home, the weather was fine and the food good. What more could a young man want? But when he landed in New York, friendless, alone, not able to understand a word of English, he felt utter confusion. Through some misunderstanding his uncle was not there to meet him when he arrived in Elk Point three days later. "In that experience I learned the first lesson of the immigrant," he once said in an interview. "The first and perhaps the greatest lesson: A feeling of utter helplessness, as if life had betrayed me. It comes from the sense of being lost in a vast alien land. In this case it was largely physical, but I soon met the spiritual phase of the same thing. The sense of being lost in an alien culture. The sense of being thrust somewhere outside the charmed circle of life. If you couldn't conquer that feeling, if you couldn't break through the magic hedge of thorns, you were lost indeed. Many couldn't, and didn't—and many were lost thereby."

The accounts of life on the farm on the South Dakota prairie as Per Smevik wrote about them to his family at home in Norway are based on the experiences of Ole Rølvaag himself. For three years he stayed at Elk Point, hoarding his money. But as soon as he had mastered his new tasks, he lost interest in them. He felt the need to improve his English, and he was dissatisfied with the intellectual life on the prairie. Though he does not intimate this in the letters of Per Smevik, Ole was greatly encouraged by a pastor in the community to seek an education. So Ole Rølvaag, then twenty-three years old, enrolled at Augustana Academy at Canton, South Dakota—a small, church-related school. These were good years for him; he received encouragement from sympathetic and idealistic teachers. He made lifelong friends. Here, too, he first met the young woman who was later to become his wife. Jennie Marie Berdahl was the daughter of a pioneer South Dakota family, and it was from her father and uncles, especially, that Rølvaag got much of the factual information which he recorded in his pioneer novels. Though he worked very hard—again he had to excel or he was not satisfied—this was an enjoyable period for him. Here he was stimulated intellectually and began a more systematic study of literature. He also had a faculty for enjoying life to the fullest. As he had been at home in Norway, he became the center of a fun-loving group here, too. Wherever he was, the conversation was livelier, the discussions flowed, and the laughter rang out. In the spring of 1901 he graduated with honors. Although there is no copy of his commencement oration, newspaper accounts told that it carried a theme which, later in life, he was to express again and again in various ways: that only by drawing on his own culture and background could the immigrant become a good American and be able to contribute to his adopted country.

Following his graduation from Augustana, he again was faced with the problem of financing his education. This time he tried his luck as a door-to-door salesman of stereopticon views—at that time a popular novelty. Though he did not record any great monetary success he said that his experiences as a salesman taught him much about human nature. He said often to his students that no one was truly educated who had not tried to sell books or aluminum-ware.

However, Ole Rølvaag had decided to enter St. Olaf College in Northfield, Minnesota. The same pastor who had encouraged him to enter Augustana now wrote to President J. N. Kildahl recommending his protégé and asking if there was an opportunity for the young man "to earn a little on the side, so that he might attend school this winter. The school would do well in making this possible, for he is a very talented young man. Hardly anyone could have passed the course of study prescribed at Canton in shorter time than he did." Ole did find work—in the dormitory kitchen, and also carrying wood to the stoves which heated the rooms in the Old Main. Years afterward, he recounted with pride the piles of wood he had carried to feed his heating stoves, and the gallons of paint he had applied to both inside and outside walls of campus buildings during vacations.

He started his studies at St. Olaf by registering for Latin, Greek, German, English composition, church history and mathematics, as well as for courses in Norwegian language and literature. The four years of college were filled with hard work. Each year he registered for extra courses in order to make up for studies he had not had opportunity for earlier, or which he, himself, felt were necessary to his own development.

Yet at St. Olaf he was not simply a drudge. Here, too, he was often the center of activity and fun. He loved the spirited debates carried on by the literary societies of his days at college; he was deeply involved in the Norwegian club *Normanna,* working hard to make his fellow students aware of their heritage. He wrote for the student newspaper and the yearbook. And on winter evenings he often relaxed with his favorite sport of skating on the river. According to a fellow student and later colleague, he believed that a student should stretch his legs and breathe pure air occasionally, and that skating was the best way of doing this.

During his junior year he began writing a novel. In letters to his future wife he described how he wrote and wrote until far into the night, neglecting his studies, he told her, in order to work on his book, for he hoped to find a publisher for it before graduating from college. The novel, *Nils og Astri,* was rejected, and although a few years later he took the manuscript out again, and polished and reworked it, it remained unpublished.

Students of his day were expected to live on campus. But Ole, being older than the average, was unwilling to stop reading and turn out his lights at ten o'clock. Besides, he found it difficult to give up his pipe, which was forbidden at school. Finally he received permission to live off campus, where he could sit up and read and smoke and write as late as he liked.

During the summer of 1902 he secured a position as a parochial school teacher in a country parish at Lime Grove, Nebraska. Besides the religious studies, the children were also taught to read and write Norwegian. Again, in the summer of 1903, he taught at Lime Grove. The summer of 1904 found him teaching at Churchs Ferry and, later, at Bisbee, North Dakota. Ole's experiences during these years are recounted in the letters of Per Smevik to his family in Norway. Ole Rølvaag was exceptionally fond of children and had a knack for winning their confidence. It must have been his satisfaction with these summer jobs that started him on a teaching career.

As commencement approached, the problem of his future became ever more pressing. Although he graduated with honors, it seems that Rølvaag was not considered by his fellow students nor by his teachers as an exceptional student. Nevertheless, President Kildahl urged the young man to study theology, while Professor Fossum wanted him to go on to do graduate work at Harvard. He, himself, was eager to find a teaching position that would enable him to marry and establish a home, to find a publisher for his novel, and to visit his old home at Dønna.

As it turned out, the Norwegian publisher to whom he sent his novel *Nils og Astri* returned the manuscript. But he was offered a position as a teacher at St. Olaf on the condition that he would first spend a year in study at the University of Kristiania (Oslo), and in July, 1905, he left for Norway.

It proved to be a year of very hard work and continuous study, hampered by ill health. But he passed his examinations with the highest grades obtainable. After the strenuous winter, he found the summer at Dønna relaxing, and of course, the reunion with his family, especially his Mother, was thrilling. He returned to St. Olaf in the fall of 1906 to begin a career which was to last a quarter of a century. That first year, it was a heavy load of teaching for the young teacher. Included on his weekly schedule were twelve hours of Norwegian, five of geometry, two of physiology, and two of geography. Soon he was relieved of the courses in physiology and geography, but instead he was to teach five hours of Greek. In addition he taught a course in Biblical history to the junior class in the academy, and he was also the resident head in the boys' dormitory.

On July 9, 1908, Ole Rølvaag and Jennie Marie Berdahl were married at her home near Garretson, South Dakota. To this union were born Olaf Arnljot, who died in childhood; Ella Valborg (Mrs. Torliff Tweet); Karl Fritjof (Governor of Minnesota, 1963-67 and U. S. Ambassador to Iceland, 1968-1970); and Paul Gunnar, who died, tragically, in childhood—drowning in a neighbor's cistern.

From the time he first began teaching until he resigned in the spring of 1931 because of poor health, Ole Rølvaag actually combined two careers—teaching and writing. He had the rare gift of understanding and sympathy for youth which helped make him a good teacher. He was extremely fond of young people and eager to help them find themselves, to encourage them to develop their talents, and to become independent in their thinking and work. Moreover he was willing to spend as much time with his students outside of class as in the classroom. He set aside special days when he was "at home," and a great many availed themselves of the opportunity to come down for a visit or to discuss their problems and aspirations with him.

He was not the kind of teacher who was content to give the same lecture, word for word, year after year. During the summers, especially, he spent a great deal of time studying, reading, and reworking material for his classes. His courses on Ibsen, and one on the history of immigration, were particularly popular.

But he was not one-sided in his interests. Books and periodicals of many kinds came almost daily to his study. Frequently he would find something he wanted to discuss with his colleagues. Then four or five of them would gather

—in his study in the winter, or out in the back yard in the summer—and they would read aloud portions of the article or book, and discuss the ideas presented.

During the last years of his life, Ole Rølvaag was deeply involved in the work of the Norwegian-American Historical Association which he helped found in 1925. Until his death, he acted as corresponding secretary, adding the demands of almost full-time work to his busy schedule of teaching and writing. He had always been an avid collector of Norwegian-American materials, and now he collected for the Historical Association's archives. As secretary, his correspondence grew by leaps and bounds.

His first published work was a matter of necessity: a Norwegian-English dictionary prepared for use by his students. There followed a series of three readers (1919, 1920, 1925), and a Norwegian grammar (1916)—all of these prepared for use by the classes in Norwegian. Some of these were written in cooperation with his colleague, Dr. P. J. Eikeland. In 1918, he edited a book of readings, including in it some original short stories and sketches. It is perhaps significant that much of the material in the readers dealt with the Norwegian-American scene and reflected the contributions of the immigrants to American life.

When *The Third Life of Per Smevik* (*Amerika-Breve*, or "Letters from America") first appeared in the late fall of 1912, the author used the pen name Paal Mørck. He confided later that the subject matter of this first novel was so personal that he felt it necessary to use a pseudonym. One can only speculate on why or how an author chooses a name. In this case we know that Mørck was a name with which he was familiar, belonging to a distant relative on his home island. Mørck, in a slightly different spelling, means "dark" in Norwegian. Paal (Paul) was a favorite name, later given to his youngest son. So, perhaps, when he felt the need of a pseudonym, it is not strange that this name occurred to him.

In the preface to the original Norwegian text, Paal Mørck tells of meeting a retired Nordland fisherman now living in South Dakota. Having gained old Mr. Smevik's confidence, he learned that the old man still had a packet of letters which his son, now a pastor in a neighboring community, wrote during his first years in this country. When Mr. Mørck was permitted to read the letters, he was fascinated by the account they gave of the gradual Americanization of a young immigrant, and was finally permitted to have the letters published. Actually, we have here a case of a double pseudonym, in that Rølvaag himself is both Paal Mørck and the young immigrant, Per Smevik. It is perhaps of interest, also, to note that Ole Rølvaag like Per Smevik, chose a place-name instead of a patronymic as a surname after his arrival in America.

Rølvaag once wrote in a letter that a novel written in the first person belongs in a special category, and demands an unusual intimacy between the writer and the story he is telling. The intimacy between the writer and the story in this case should be apparent since the story is largely autobiographical. Rølvaag had asked his older brother Johan (the Andreas of the story) to write a literary criticism of the book. Almost immediately the return letter came—fourteen closely-written pages. "Of all types of fiction, the novel in letter form is certainly the worst," wrote the brother, "unless it be the one in diary form. The author must have an eye on each finger, so to speak, or he will become repetitious and trivial. You have cleared this hurdle well . . . . As far as subject matters goes—these are merely the letters you have writen home to Father and to me. So you will have to admit that this time your task was an easy one."

The novel received favorable reviews; one writer maintained that if an immigrant had neglected writing home, he could now send this volume to his family in Norway, and they would have a picture of life in America as experienced by the newcomer.

Two years later Rølvaag dropped his use of the pseudonym and a second novel *Paa Glemte Veie* (On Forgotten Paths) was published under his own name by a Minneapolis publisher. In 1920, he completed *To Tullinger* (Two Fools) which was substantially rewritten and translated as "Pure Gold" in 1931; and in 1921 came *Laengselens Baat* (The Boat of Longing) which appeared in an English translation in 1933. These books were published in the United States, and circulated among his people in this country. *For Faedrearven* (Concerning Our Heritage) which was published in 1922, is a volume of essays, polemical in nature, dealing with his program for his people, namely the preservation of heritage as a means of strengthening their cultural life as well as adding dimension to their contribution as Americans.

Then in 1923, Rølvaag learned that a Norwegian novelist intended to visit the United States and write a book about the Norwegian immigrants here. This spurred him on to work on a long-planned novel which became *Giants in the Earth,* but was first published in Norway (1925) in two volumes as *I de dage* (In Those Days), and *Riket grundlegges* (The Founding of the Kingdom).

With the exception of a few brief excerpts of a planned autobiography, articles and lectures, Rølvaag preferred to write in Norwegian rather than in English. He maintained that Joseph Conrad was the only one of the few non-native English writers who could write beautifully in his adopted language. For Rølvaag said often that for him "the words must sing," and he felt that he could make them sing only in his native Norwegian. However, when *Giants in the Earth* was translated into English, he took an active part in the final preparation of the manuscript, working closely with

Mr. Lincoln Colcord, who helped put it in its final artistic form. The publication of *Giants in the Earth* brought him fame as an artist, both in Norway and the United States. The novel was a selection of the Book-of-the-Month Club in 1927. *Peder Victorious* and *Their Father's God* followed in English translations in 1929 and 1931. So we have the rather strange phenomenon of an American citizen writing on an American theme in a foreign language.

The pressure of teaching, added to the other work which he took on—working with his students; lecturing; supporting the college in every way possible, even to giving up part of a sorely-needed sabbatical leave in order to solicit funds for the school after a disastrous fire had destroyed one of its buildings; carrying on a voluminous correspondence—all made it necessary for him to seek seclusion for his writing. He could find solitude in many places—on shipboard, in a hotel in London, at home in Northfield, where he established a routine for his work, but best of all was the solitude he found in the woods of northern Minnesota. In Itasca County, on the shore of a small lake, he built a modest cabin, and there the family spent many summers. At Big Island life soon settled into a routine: several hours of steady writing in the forenoon, followed by a morning dip in the lake when the weather was warm; lunch on the sunny porch, followed by a short rest, during which his wife usually read aloud from a book or magazine. If she thought he seemed to have fallen asleep, and stopped reading, he nearly always opened one eye, and said, "Go on, go on, I'm listening." A relaxing hand or two of honeymoon bridge preceded several hours of steady work at the table. In the evening, when the lamp was lit, the whole family gathered around the big table, Rølvaag with his writing, the others with books or handwork. The stacks of yellow copy paper, written and rewritten, scratched out and written again, grew higher as the summer progressed. Fishing in the early evening was a regular part of the day's activities. Occasionally there was a hike through the woods, a visit with an old friend for a game of chess, or a picnic or blueberrying expedition—simple pleasures through which he gained strength for the coming year, when he added the teaching load to his self-imposed schedule of writing. During the school year he often had to work far into the night, especially if he was having a difficult time getting his "characters to behave" as he himself put it. His family had the feeling that he was working against time—and that he was, too, for the first copy of *Their Father's God* reached him only a few days before his death. He intimated that he had plans for another book about the Holm family, but that was not to be.

During the late 1920s he had a series of heart attacks of increasing severity. He had to give up skating on the river with his children. He had to give up golf, because he could not learn to walk slowly around the course. But he could not give up his work. Nor could he learn to take his work at an easier pace. There is a family legend about a great-great grandfather, who was once chided for going at things so hard. "I'd rather live while I live, and die a fortnight earlier" was his rejoinder. A little of the same spirit imbued Ole Rølvaag. He could never tackle anything in a half-hearted manner.

"Skål for the impossible!" he once wrote. Certainly that was his motto. "Skål for the impossible!"—that was the way to achieve one's highest purpose in life. And there *was* purpose to life, of that he was convinced. Therefore he had to work harder in order to reach his goal and finish his appointed work in time.

In October, 1931, he suffered another severe heart attack, and at the age of fifty-five, died on November 5 at his home in Northfield.

—Ella Valborg Tweet

1896 First Impressions

Clarkfield, South Dakota
August 26, 1896

Dear Father,

Here I am at last! And now I must try to write. The worst of it is, I don't know where to begin and where to end. It's not quite a month since I left home, but it seems like an eternity — and a long one at that! It is as if I have already lived two lives here on earth: the first was in Smeviken, and that lasted almost twenty-one years. The second one I lived through on the trip from Smeviken in Helgeland to Clarkfield, South Dakota. Now I am about to begin a third. Strangely enough, although the second life lasted only a little more than three weeks, it seemed much longer than the first. God alone knows how long the third will last or how long it will seem, and only He knows if I will ever experience a fourth life!

These were my thoughts this morning when Uncle Hans woke me with, "Now you must get up and have some 'brakkfest'." "Brakkfest" is English, of course, but what it means, I haven't the slightest idea. I thought it must be something to eat but I can't imagine what kind of food it is. All we had was bread, butter, eggs, fried pork and coffee — and something strange in a glass, which we spread on our bread. It was sweet and awfully good. Perhaps that's what is called "brakkfest." I didn't like to ask about it, you see, because it seemed so dumb not to understand such a simple word. In Norwegian, I suppose we would have called it "American syrup." Oh well, I'll find out sometime.

Uncle Hans looks about the same as he did when he left us twelve years ago. He has kept house for the same man for eleven years now, and believe me, he is good at it; the house is so clean and tidy that the rooms fairly shine. And such good meals he makes! But then he has plenty to work with; there is certainly no shortage of supplies here. Uncle Hans says that he has arranged with his boss to let me stay here for the first few weeks so I can get my bearings before I look for a job. He certainly must realize that I can't afford to spend two weeks doing nothing — that I have come to America to make money! However I thought it best not to say anything just yet.

America is surely a strange country. Would you believe that the *men* do all the chores? They don't get out of it even on Sunday. I wonder if I will have to milk. Well, if they demand that of me, then ——! That isn't so unlikely either; the boss teased me this evening by saying that he wouldn't expect me to milk all seventeen cows — not tonight, at least. But he hinted that if I'm going to stay in America I will certainly have to learn how. Well, "That's some butter," as the old lady in the fairy tale said when she got lard on her bread. I simply will not do it. Imagine! A grown man sitting down to pull at cow teats, a man as dairy maid, as *chore boy!*

I know, of course, that on some of the big farms in Norway hired men worked in the barns, but they were the laughing stock of all the young people and we called them names that certainly aren't found in any Bible. No, before I do that kind of work I'll give myself up to the Indians.

(Haven't seen any Indians yet, even though I have traveled across most of America. This seems quite odd. From all the Indian stories we read at home I should have thought that every grove would be swarming with them.)

But now I absolutely can't write any more. I'm still tired from the trip and my eyes won't stay open any longer. I'll write to Andreas and tell about my trip. That will be a terribly long letter, so I thought I'd write a little each evening until the story is told. Hope this finds you all well, and that you have already written.

Your devoted son,
Peder Andersen

My address is: P. Andersen
Clarkfield P. O.
Beaker County, South Dakota
U.S.A.

Clarkfield, South Dakota
September 2, 1896

DEAR BROTHER,

If I'd had any idea how much I would see and experience on my trip over I would never have promised to write about everything, for that would fill a book. In fact I doubt that I could get it all into one volume. It certainly seems as if no one has time to write books in America, not the men anyway. I haven't seen many women yet, so I don't know if they can write books.

It is absolutely impossible for me to describe how I felt as I stood alone on the pier and watched the boys sail home in that boat I was so fond of—well, fond of the boys too, of course. I assure you that at that moment I had no more desire to go to America than I had to throw myself right into the sea. As a matter of fact, I've never had any great longing for America.

But, there I stood on the pier and stared after the boys and the boat until they had completely disappeared behind Skarvholmen on the other side of the fjord. When the last corner of the square sail was gone, I felt as if a door closed within me and a room was locked forever. But people were coming and going on the dock and I couldn't stand there gaping like a fool, so I sauntered up to the store and went in as if there were nothing at all the matter with me. Can you guess what I did then? I went right up to the counter and bought a neat little pipe and half a pound of shredded Langaard's tobacco. You remember I quit smoking last winter at Lofoten and haven't had so much as a taste since, but I got so desperately lonesome as I stood around waiting for the coastal steamer that I had to do something. So I sat and smoked. Perhaps I shouldn't have done it for now you shall hear what happened.

This tobacco lasted me most of the trip, until the second day on the train from New York to South Dakota. By that time there was nothing left but the crust in my pipe. It was lonely enough to walk about there on the pier waiting for the boat, but it was ten times worse to sit in that crowded train hour after hour, watching the endless bustle of people getting on and off, and listening to the incessant drone of voices without understanding a single word. Well yes, I did hear the word "money" many times and I knew at least that much English. I had noticed that every once in a while a young fellow in a uniform, a regular dandy, came through the car with a basket full of all kinds of good things which he sold to the passengers. In the basket he had the nicest looking apples and oranges, and many other fruits and good things that I did not recognize. I surely would have liked some of those too, but even more I wanted a good pipeful of tobacco. So once when he came past me, I resolutely grabbed hold of his leg. Then he had to stop, you see. I held out my pipe and made signs that I wanted something in it. Yes indeed. He understood Norwegian remarkably well. He sat down beside me and from his basket brought out a beautiful packet all wrapped up in silver paper. They must have plenty of money here in this country. Now the question was how much did this packet cost? I asked in Norwegian, but he only shook his head and laughed. So I held up one hand and stretched out all five fingers, but do you suppose that was enough? Oh no! He immediately held up both hands and I understood that he wanted ten for it, but ten of what I had no idea. I brought out the only American coin I had left, and on it was written "one dime." This and a Norwegian five-øre piece was all the money I had. As soon as I showed him the coin, he grinned in approval, so I gave it to him and took the packet.

True enough, I'd had no food for a day and a half except a bit of dry bread, and now that was all gone; and I didn't know how much longer it would be before I arrived. But I also knew from previous experience that tobacco silences hunger pangs rather well. Besides I had gone without food for as long as three whole days and survived, so I supposed I could survive this time too. If worst came to worst, I still had the five-øre piece. It has the Norwegian crown on it and surely must be worth something even in this foreign land. I took the tobacco and the fellow even gave me a box of matches besides. Well, the package turned out to be better in appearance than in reality. The tobacco was dry as dust so it burned too fast and made my tongue sore. Not all products are first class in America.

But now I can't write any more tonight. I think I have already written a lot. This week I've just rested and tried to learn a little of this and that on the farm. Tomorrow we begin haying, and then I'll have a real job, and be paid full wages. Goodnight for now.

September 3

Believe me, today I have been put to the test! I was up with the hired man at daybreak, helped him as well as I could with the barn chores, and most of the day tried to do my share. Was it hard work! And so hot—especially late in the afternoon. I could feel the sweat running all the way down into my shoes. As luck would have it, towards five o'clock my nose began to bleed and even though I stuffed grass into both nostrils I could not get it to stop. There was nothing else for me to do but quit working. I can't tell you how disgusted I was that I couldn't last the whole day. I wanted to show these fellows that I was just as good a worker as any of them, which they certainly won't believe now. I am positive they talked about me as I went home, that I could understand from a few words I heard, even if I don't know any English. But just wait! The day will come when I'll do my share as well as any one of them, and perhaps even a little better. This evening, however, I ache in every joint and my hand shakes so I can scarcely hold the pen. You can see that in America life is not all leisure. I'll write about the work and everything else later.

Before I crawl into bed I'll tell you about how I found Uncle Hans. It was like this: You remember how Uncle always wrote "Peary P.O." in his address? I thought this must be the name of the farm he worked on. Now I know better. In America, you see, farms don't have any names. How do they keep things straight then? I wish I knew! I'll explain that later when I've had a chance to find out. "Peary P.O." is the name of the post office where he gets his mail, and is seven English miles from the farm where he works. Uncle Hans wrote in his last letter that I should get off the train in Clarkfield, and he would meet me at the station.

September 4

Saturday evening the twenty-fifth of August, three days after I got on the train in New York, I was put off in Clarkfield. Actually, I should have said thrown off, for the immigrant is handled like a piece of freight; he is pushed and shoved and pointed along, sometimes he is even kicked and pinched forward—that I saw in New York. If I had gotten that kind of treatment you can bet I would have pinched back! But what can you do when you are in a strange country and you don't understand a syllable of what is said, and where everything moves like lightning? You just have to bite your tongue and take it, and be thankful to get where you are going.

As soon as I came out on the platform I began to look around for Uncle Hans, or for someone who resembled the picture of him I had in my mind's eye. Every now and then I stepped forward thinking I saw a familiar face. There must have been two or three hundred people at the station, so that made it easier to make a mistake. Little by little the crowd thinned out, but still no Uncle Hans. Each time I mustered up enough courage to greet someone with a face that could have been his, I got only a surprised smile and a shake of the head. Stones for bread is a poor diet, but smiles and strange faces instead of uncles is certainly not much better—especially towards evening in a strange place when one is dead tired and has only an old Norwegian five-øre piece in his pocket. One by one, the people disappeared until at last I stood there alone.

Then and there I could have used some good advice. Finally an official came out and spoke to me; he used both words and gestures, but still I couldn't make out a single syllable of what he said. English is certainly difficult to understand. After he had gone back inside I sat right down on the station platform and began to study the situation. Perhaps Uncle Hans would come later? It could be that the train had been early, for it had gone at breakneck speed at times. Well, there I sat and pondered. It came to me as a comforting thought that Uncle Hans must be somewhere nearby.

While I sat there thinking about my problem, I saw six men come walking along the tracks toward the station. They carried spades and pickaxes over their shoulders, and tin pails in their hands. I could tell by their clothes they were working men. Suddenly the thought struck me that one of these must be Uncle Hans. As they came nearer I took special notice of a tall fair man with a blond mustache. My heart pounded with joy. It's true, the man looked somewhat older than I expected Uncle Hans to look, but then I knew that people aged faster over here in this country. When they got close I stood up and greeted them politely, but they just nodded and went on into the station. Then my heart sank! The sun was already setting and by now I was so hungry my stomach growled and I was terribly thirsty as well. This began to look very strange.

Suddenly the blond man came out again and walked over to me. Without further ceremony he asked in Swedish, "Are you Scandinavian?" I would never have believed I could be so happy to see a Swede. And I can assure you that never have words sounded sweeter than those Swedish words sounded to me then. I could have hugged that good-hearted fellow right on the spot. I began to explain that I was on my way to Peary P.O., and that I had an Uncle named Hans Hansen, or Hans Hansen Smevik. Did he know him?—No, he had never heard of him.—Well, that didn't matter; if I could only get directions to Peary, I could certainly find my way from there.—But it's more than seven miles.—Oh, that was nothing! Seven, eight English miles were only a little more than one Norwegian mile, and to walk one Norwegian mile was nothing, even if I was tired. At least that's what I thought then. He didn't know the way but could easily find out, and back into the station he went to get directions. Soon he returned and explained carefully: I was to walk two miles straight that way and then I would come to a crossroad; from there I must go north exactly four miles; there I would find another crossroad; then I should go west. It was only one and a half miles to Peary from that corner. Clearly and distinctly he repeated the entire explanation; slowly and carefully I said each word after him to fasten them even better in my memory. Thereupon I thanked him heartily for the information.

Just as I was about to start off, he asked in Swedish, "Are you very hungry?" I felt my face turn red. I had never begged for food, but—this was not exactly begging. In my best Swedish, I stammered bashfully, "Yes, I'm rather hungry." At this the Swede laughed heartily, went into the station, and came out again with his tin pail. From it he took some bread and butter and a bottle half-full of cold coffee. "If you're that hungry, I think this will go down!" With these words he handed me both the sandwich and the coffee. And down it went. I drank the coffee in one gulp and the sandwich quickly followed. Again I said good-bye, this time even more heartily. "God bless his good Swedish heart," I said to myself many times as I walked along the country road. And now I shall ask one thing of you, Andreas, and you must ask Mother and Father too: Whenever a Swede comes drifting in to Smeviken, as so often happens, be kind to him, no matter how ragged and dirty he is. Don't forget!

As I trudged along the road, my courage rose several degrees. Life was not so bad after all. It's wonderful how a friendly Swede with a sandwich and a little cold coffee can brighten the outlook of a tired and hungry young man. I was in such good humor that I began to whistle as I hurried along. It was so stifling hot that first I shed my coat, then the vest. My shirt was unpardonably dirty, but that was no wonder for I hadn't had it off since I put it on in Smeviken. Fortunately dusk was coming on, so if I happened to meet someone it wouldn't be noticed anyway.

Well, I said it was fortunate dusk was coming on—but actually it was unfortunate because it got dark so terribly fast which I should have known had I given it any thought. But it's not always so easy to keep everything in mind. It was almost completely dark by the time I reached the first crossroad. Sure enough, there were four roads, and here I was to go north. But now I was in a fix. Believe it or not, I couldn't decide which way was north! Of course you will think this was stupid of me, but I assure you that the same thing would have happened to you. Suddenly the thought struck me that surely the sun must set in the west here just as it does everywhere else, and I scanned the horizon to see where the sun had gone down. It had already set but on the horizon to the northeast (or what I thought was northeast) there was still a faint streak of red. The only conclusion I could draw from this was that in America the sun sets in the north or northeast. It makes me laugh now, when I think back on my stupidity. Anyway I took the road that I thought went north, but which actually led west.

By now I had walked two miles, so there should be less than six left. But what a landscape! I know you won't believe this, but it was flat as the flattest floor in our house at home. I could see no houses anywhere, only endless fields and meadows. Some of the fields were freshly plowed; others seemed to have just been cut, for there were shocks of grain in long rows as far as the eye could see. My feet were beginning to hurt so I took off my shoes and socks. Then I really put on speed! I walked and walked, and occasionally I ran. I wanted to reach Uncle Hans's place before everyone went to bed. Once after having raced along for quite a distance I stopped to catch my breath and rest awhile. This was beginning to wear me out.

It had been completely dark for some time. The stars twinkled and shone brightly, and that seemed to give me courage—although I can't really say I was afraid either. But good heavens! There was the North Star directly to the east! This made me so discouraged and upset that I sat right down in the middle of the road. The only conclusion I could draw from this was that either the North Star was off course, or the sun was, or I was. And no matter how much I disliked the idea, I had to admit that I was the one. What I had taken for north or northeast was west, just as it ought to have been. Instead of going north at the first crossroads, I had gone west. The North Star can be depended upon, this I knew from that dreadful night when we sailed from Fleinvær to Værøy without a compass. My situation now was not much better. At this moment I would gladly have traded a stormy night on the Vestfjord for this summer night on the prairie. Now what should I do? Should I walk back to the last crossroads? That would take at least three quarters of an hour or more, as tired as I was. Or should I continue along this road until I found people, for there must be some people in the vicinity; there were, after all, cultivated fields all around. My legs ached and I was so exhausted that I chose the latter. This road would just have to lead wherever and to whomever it would. If necessary I could always sneak into a barn and sleep in the hay.

I walked more slowly now to save my strength so I could hold out longer. For the first time I noticed that the night was alive around me; I heard a steady monotonous humming and buzzing. It whirred and whirred and whirred all around me. Suddenly I stopped dead in my tracks. "Indians!" I thought. "Now you'll see, in a moment they'll take your scalp!" I might as well admit it; at that moment, I was scared. Instinctively I felt back on my hip for my sheath knife, but of course it was in my trunk. Soon I realized that it couldn't possibly be redskins, because the sound was too steady and monotonous, and it blended so well into the darkness around me. It seemed to come from every straw and stem and from every particle of dust in the air. (Uncle Hans told me later it was insects I heard.)

I calmed down after I gave up all thoughts of scalping and even began to whistle a little. Imagine my joy when suddenly I saw a light by the side of the road not far ahead of me. Maybe there were Norwegians living there? Then there would be both food and a bed for me and I could find out the way to Uncle Hans and amble over in the morning. How wonderful it would be to crawl into bed. In high spirits I sat down on the edge of the road and pulled on my shoes and socks; it would never do to come in barefooted.

Soon I reached the house. With my heart in my throat, I knocked on the door. "Come in," called a man's deep voice from within. Hmm, this sounded just like Norwegian. Boldly I opened the door and stepped in. Coming in from the dark I was blinded by the bright light, so it took a moment before I could get my bearings and say hello properly. The family sat around the table eating supper. In response to my greeting, I got nothing but blank looks. Some of them sat there staring at me with their mouths full of half-chewed food. I thought perhaps they had not understood me so I repeated my greeting, slowly and distinctly. I even added "Bless the food" so they might know that I was properly brought up, and not just a common tramp.

The man just shook his head and said something that I couldn't understand.

Of course I got flustered, especially when I looked around the room and saw how elegant everything was. But they all looked so kind that I took courage and began to explain and gesture. First I mentioned Peary, and then pointed this way and that. Yes, the man understood me. And he began to talk and to point, point and talk, but I understood nothing except the pointing—and not much of that either, for first he pointed here and then there, until he had pointed to all the corners of the earth. I thought, however, that he meant I could either go back to the crossroad where I had gone wrong, and go north from there, or else I could continue on to the next crossroad, and go north and then east.

It was easy enough for him to sit before a table full of food and point to the four corners of the earth, not quite so easy for me to get there. Oh, how tempted I was to ask for food. And that I could have gotten him to understand, too, but I have never begged and I never will either. I'd croak first. With a longing look at the food that would have brought tears to the eye of any kind hearted Nordlander, I said "Thank you" and "Good night." With that I left. (Uncle told me today this was an Irish family.)

It seemed even darker when I came out again. What in the world should I do now? I wanted more than anything else to lie right down there by the side of the road and sleep for now I was dead tired. I might have done it too, if it hadn't been for my stomach; it literally gnawed down there under my ribs, I was so hungry. The Swede's coffee and sandwich had long since disappeared.

After thinking it over awhile I decided it was best to continue on in the same direction. Again I took off my coat and vest and set out. I walked and walked. My feet were tender and sore, but I trudged on just the same. At last I was so tired I just had to sit down. Although the grass at the side of the road was stiff and tall, it was a great relief to stretch out and rest there. And do you know what I saw as I lay there? No, Andreas, I doubt that you do, for I saw Smeviken! It seemed as though I lay on the hillside in front of our house. I saw the bay lying mirror-like before me; now and then there was a rippling in the water. And as clear as day I could see our boat (yours, I suppose I should say now) moored there, and could even hear the lapping of the waves as they reached the boat and slapped gently against the sides. I would have given any one of my limbs at that moment if I could have traded the vision for reality.

Finally I became so melancholy that I sat up, reached for my pipe, and began to smoke. No, it wasn't the smartest thing to do, you're right about that, but then we don't always live according to reason.

Suddenly I awoke from my reverie when the grass rustled beside me. In spite of my weariness I shot up and listened breathlessly. No sound came. That was strange, I thought, so I struck a match and looked down at the ground. This time, I tell you, your brother was scared—for there lay a snake coiled up right beside me. It raised its head, flicked its tongue in and out, and hissed horribly. I didn't stick around there very long, you may be sure! I ran—no, flew down the road. Every now and then I thought I heard a rustling in the grass, first on one side of the road and then the other. I ran and ran for at least a quarter of an hour until I couldn't take it any longer, and had to slow down to a walk. Little by little that dreadful fear left me but as the fear left, the tiredness returned. I dragged one foot after the other. Oh how sore they were! Each step was torture. Now after seeing the snake, I didn't dare take my shoes off again.

In the midst of my weariness the thought came to me that perhaps this was to be my last night on earth. I went so far as to begin to make my peace with God. I can't say that I felt any special fear of death. It just seemed so ironic that I should die of exhaustion and hunger, right here in the promised land—and then likely be eaten up by serpents, too. And it was too bad to die now, just as I was about to begin a new life.

These sad thoughts were suddenly interrupted when a short distance ahead of me I saw the silhouette of a house against the dark night sky. In front of the house a man was working with a team of horses and a wagon; it looked as if he were just hitching up. I went up to him, and as boldly as I could, said "Good evening." I assure you that when he answered in broad Trondheim dialect, I was so happy that I was close to tears. It sounds silly, I know, but I doubt that even you would have felt any different. Could he tell me the way to Peary? Oh yes, I had a straight road from the corner here to Peary. (For "road" he used a word I had never heard, but I understood what he meant.) And now I noticed that I stood right at a crossroads.—How far was it?—About six miles.— Six miles! Did he know a man hereabouts by the name of Hans Hansen?—Yes, of course. He knew him very well. I could have hugged that man, I was so happy.—Did he live far from here?—About five miles. —That far?—Yes, was I looking for him?—Yes. Then I told him who I was, that I had just come from Norway, that Hans Hansen was my uncle.—Well then, I could just sit up beside him on the wagon, for he was driving right past the place on his way home. I didn't say much on that ride, though the Trondheimer asked and asked for news from Norway. I just sat there the whole time and wondered what good deed I could do for this man, or how I could best show my gratitude when I became rich.

We arrived there safe and sound. Uncle Hans was so happy that he nearly cried when I came. He hadn't expected me in Clarkfield until the next day, and had all the time worried that I would get lost. I came in and washed up, and was given good food also, but best of all was certainly the bed. And that's where I am headed now, for it is way past midnight. I have been writing this letter for four nights, and it is almost a book. I'll put three stamps on it to make sure it gets there. I have written so much because both you and Father warned me not to do as the others who went to America, and never bothered to write home.

You will have to read this letter to Mother and Father. Hearty greetings to you all, especially Mother!

Your loving brother,
Peder Andersen Smevik

P.S. Next time I will write to Father. I plan to change about and write one letter to you and the next to him. Don't forget to tell all about the summer herring, both the net fishing and the trawling. Uncle Hans sends greetings.

P.A.S.

Clarkfield, South Dakota
September 11, 1896

DEAR ANDREAS,

How are you, Brother? Here comes a letter from America. Actually this one should have been addressed to Father, but I don't suppose it matters who gets the letter, just so someone does. You know I have to be careful when I write to Father; though he is only a fisherman, he has had some education, and is very critical, but to you I can fire away as I please.

I hope this letter finds you in the best of health and victorious in your fight with the cod. How many of those fellows have you nabbed since I left you this summer? Yes, summer! For it is still summer here even though it is the middle of September, and so hot during the day that I am tempted to wear only my birthday suit.

America is certainly a peculiar country. Here everything is topsy-turvy. Take the summer for example. Even this late in the season it is hotter than in the middle of July at home in Smeviken. By eight o'clock in the evening it is already dark as night. The food and mealtimes are even more upside-down. Here they eat only three times a day, but the evening meal does come as early as six o'clock. The food is very good, mostly meat and potatoes, white bread and jam. Bread and butter is served at every meal, and so is coffee. They have such curious names for their meals. Even Uncle Hans, whose dialect is the same as mine, calls the evening meal "supper," the noon meal "dinner," and the morning meal "breakfast." Yes, now I know what Uncle Hans meant that first morning when he told me to get up and have some "brakkfest." And I thought it was some kind of food!

So it is with other things too, especially the names of dishes, tools and even buildings. It is almost impossible to know what they mean. Uncle Hans calls some of the dishes we use "plait" and "pitsher"; the stove is "stoven," monkey wrench is "maunkirenshen," the cowshed is "barn," and the summer kitchen is "kukshenti." Of course this is English, so you see I have learned quite a bit already. But don't you ever believe that this is all I have learned in these two weeks. I bet I could come up with at least a hundred words if I wanted to, but that would give you no pleasure. However I can't say I like their way of talking; they could just as well use Norwegian words when they speak Norwegian. But they don't do that; they stick in English words here and there. If Uncle Hans came home now and spoke Norwegian the way he does here, you would think it was English and I am sure you couldn't possibly understand all he said.

It is very embarrassing when Uncle Hans tells me to do something; I stand there like a fool—a real nincompoop who can't understand a thing. I know very well that I'm not dumb, but they don't know that here. This evening Uncle Hans told me to "Take this 'svill peil' and 'slabba pigsa'." That stumped me. I did understand "pigsa" meant the pigs, but "svill peil" and "slabba" were beyond me. Even such a smart fellow as you think you are could not have understood that command. Well, in good Norwegian we would say, "Take this swill pail and feed the pigs." That is what it means!

When I began this letter I intended to tell you a little about my trip over. I saw and heard so much it's hard to know where to begin and where to end. I must try to tell a little anyway.

The trip to Trondheim on the coastal steamer was fine. There was nothing left of my lunch when I got there and I was desperately hungry, as usual. My, what a big city I thought it was. You remember how you and Father warned me to be careful and not get lost in the big cities. It was good advice indeed. And if you ever intend to venture out into the world I beg you to heed the same advice. Never mind wrinkling your nose at that, even though you have been to Tromsø, Hammerfest, and Vardø. I assure you, and I mean no slight by it, those towns of yours up North are only dinky little burgs; not even a baby could get lost there.

But come to Chicago! Or New York! There you would have to follow your own advice. I was pretty careful in Trondheim; each time I went out, I noted the streets and paid particular attention to the corners and signs. All went well as long as I was in Norway where I could read; it wasn't quite so easy here where I couldn't understand a word.

The trip by train from Trondheim to Oslo was interesting. I saw much that was beautiful. The fine, broad country around Lake Mjøsa impressed me as it lay there smiling in the sun. I thought Eidsvoll the most beautiful place I saw on this trip. But mountains? No, to see mountains there is no other place to go but to Nordland.

Oslo seemed awfully big, much bigger than Trondheim. I saw neither the King nor the Queen, nor do I care much; expect they were in Sweden at the time. I am a republican now and have lost all interest in kings.

At the emigrant hotel in Oslo I met two Swedes who were also going to America. One was from Gothenburg, the other from Värmland. We were assigned to the same room and soon became good friends. They had been in the city two whole days before I came, and one of them was born and raised in Gothenburg—a really big city, he said. We spent the two days we had in the city tramping around with the Gothenburger as pilot. The last day he got the notion that we should see the art gallery. I agreed heartily without having the slightest idea what that might be. We started off in the afternoon and found the place without much trouble, thanks to the Gothenburger's perserverance in asking.

You have never seen an art gallery, Brother, and it is just as well if you never do, for frankly I can't say it was particularly uplifting. One grayish stone figure after another stood along all the walls. These figures were life-size and without a stitch of clothing on their bodies. I was dreadfully embarrassed but pretended it was nothing. I walked around in the crowd (there must have been a whole church full) and looked at those figures as if I had done nothing else in all my life but walk around among naked people. If only that Värmlander had been just as bold, but he certainly wasn't. He began to snicker as soon as we came in, and to make all kinds of indecent remarks. It didn't get really bad until we came to a giant of a fellow. A large group of men and women dressed in velvets and furs were looking at this same figure. Such shamelessness was too much for the Värmlander's honest heart. At first he only chuckled good-naturedly, but the laughter soon got the best of him. He stood doubled up, his hands on his knees and laughed until the tears rolled. Before long everyone was staring at him. I was so ashamed I could have sunk through the floor, and sneaked away as fast as I could. I didn't see him again until I went to bed that night. He was still laughing. I can't quite see why people want to show anything like that; it certainly doesn't do any good.

Oh what weeping and wailing on the pier at Oslo when the ship was ready to sail. It was enough to make one hate the thought of America. We sailed out through the Oslo fjord in the most delightful weather and in the early evening reached Kristiansand where we lay until the next forenoon. Then we set out to sea. The next landing place was to be New York. I stood on deck all afternoon. The mountains sank lower and lower into the horizon as the day waned. When nothing more could be seen but a low, rugged cloud bank, I went below, crept into my bunk and bawled like a whipped child. That was my farewell to the Fatherland.

The days on the ocean were the most glorious I have ever spent. I never expect to experience such luxury again. There was plenty to eat and the food was fairly good. The sea rolled just enough for good sleep. We had only a couple of nasty days, scarcely worth mentioning, but my goodness how sick some of those landlubbers were! I can't quite see what made them sick, for with the kind of vessel we were on I considered this fine weather and smooth sailing. Anyhow, we who were well gained by the others being sick because we got all the food we could chuck into ourselves. Of course it was gluttony, but would it have been less sinful to have thrown all that good food overboard into the sea?

I shall never forget sailing into New York—not even if I get to be twice as old as the oldest man in the Bible—which I really don't wish for in this heat. Not even if I were as good a poet as Petter Dass could I describe the sight of the city as we sailed up the Hudson River at sunrise on that sparkling morning. Sure as I'm sitting here writing this letter, I didn't come to my senses until we landed at the pier. Do you remember when Lars Johansen came home from America last winter, how we all declared he lied when he told about New York? I'll tell you what was the matter with him: he didn't lie enough! By that I mean he did not exaggerate in the least. We landed in the morning and by evening I was on the train heading for Clarkfield. Isn't it strange that of all the people I saw on board ship not one of them was on the train with me?

With this I had better close. How I got along on the train and how I found Uncle Hans's place, you already know. Now you have the story of my trip to America. But if you are not just as faithful in return and tell me about absolutely everything from home, you will have to deal with me when I get back. Just remember that.

Your devoted brother,
Per Smevik

Clarkfield, South Dakota
September 25, 1896

DEAR FATHER,

It is already two weeks since I wrote to Andreas, and as it's Sunday evening and I'm not especially tired, I'll scratch off a few lines to you. I do hope you folks on the other side of the Atlantic are as faithful about writing as I am on my side. I am longing intensely for letters and news from home. My boss takes a Norwegian newspaper, printed here in this country; it's called *Skandinaven,* and each week it has news from Norway, but so far I haven't found anything from Helgeland and naturally nothing from Smeviken.

Today I have been to church for the second time since I came here. Church customs are quite different here and so very strange that I must try to tell you a little about them. I rather think that you, Father, who have always been somewhat dissatisfied with the State Church, would like this free church better. I like it myself in many respects, but I must confess there is much I do not like. The pastors in this country don't act like big shots. No one can say that about them, at least not about the one we have here.

Uncle Hans and I waited until after the service was over and then he just about dragged me up to shake hands with the pastor who was just as common and democratic as a fisherman from Nordland, perhaps even more so. He chatted and asked me about all kinds of things. I got the impression there was very little clerical about him; he wore neither robe nor collar nor anything of that sort. In fact, when I heard his sermon it reminded me of the lay preachers at home. As far as I could tell he preached God's word, pure and simple.

It was Confirmation Day, and the young people to be

confirmed seemed quite bright; most of them, at least, knew as much as I did when I got through. The pastor didn't seem to be so well satisfied though, for in his sermon he scolded the parents severely because the children did no better. He said right out from the pulpit that this was the worst confirmation class he had ever had. I suppose this has to be just as first-rate as everything else in America, and so more than ordinary preparation is necessary in order to be catechized. I'm just glad I was confirmed in Norway. I surely wouldn't like to be scolded like that before an entire congregation just because I didn't have the catechism at the tip of my tongue. As I said, everything has to be first-rate here in this country.

The church itself is a small wooden building but very attractive inside. And yet I felt there wasn't the same air of solemnity in it as in our venerable old stone church at home.

You should have seen how dressed up the folks were. You never saw anything like it! The women, even wrinkled old women of seventy or eighty, wore hats loaded with pretty flowers. There must be a lot of extravagance in America, judging by appearances. As a matter of fact the men, too, were well dressed. But the children and the girls—the way they were decked out was downright scandalous. They looked like our finest rich folks at home. I can't say they were so pretty anyway; they looked pale and sickly, as if they hadn't had a smell of the Lord's blessed sun and rain and wind.

I didn't see a single person who walked to church. No, they all drove, some with one horse but most with two. And the rigs they had! The harnesses and the buggies were so elegant and polished they shone from far off. Neither the sheriff nor the district judge in Norway has such fine equipage. If this isn't pride and vanity, then I don't know what is. I was thoroughly convinced of this, because as soon as we came home we boys had to get out of our best clothes and go out to do chores. There hadn't been time to clean the barn before we left in the morning and so we had to do it right in the middle of Sunday while we waited for dinner. It took exactly one hour of hard, sweaty work, and this just after we had come from God's House. I can't understand that it is worthwhile playing big shot in fancy clothes when one hasn't the means to do so all the time.

From this you can see that I had to become a chore boy after all. Oh yes, I just have to come along nicely and help milk, shovel manure, and take care of the pigs too. You don't need to let this get out among my friends at home. After all, they don't know anything about conditions here, and that I am obliged to do this work. This evening I milked no less than eight cows. Uncle Hans took the other nine. The two of us had to do all the chores because the boss and the other hired man were out visiting. It took us a little more than two and a half hours to finish. First we milked all seventeen cows, then I fed and watered the pigs and the horses (eighty-five pigs and seven horses) while Uncle Hans separated the milk. I must admit, though, that I find this work rather interesting. I don't think it would hurt in the least if young people at home had a chance to learn some of it. Besides I can't see, when I think it over, that it is any worse to grub in cow manure than in fish guts and such things, as the fellows at home have to do. I don't mind doing this work on weekdays, but on Sundays it is quite different.

As I sat milking tonight, I got to thinking about our summer evenings at home and the good times we used to have up on the Smevik ridge and in the Lia glen, until I became quite depressed. Oh well, that's the way it is in this world: nothing is gained but that something is lost.

I have already earned fourteen dollars in a little more than three weeks. That makes fifty-one kroner and eighty øre which I think is pretty good. Now I'm going to try to get some day work for the fall season. I've considered hiring out to a threshing crew; that pays extremely well, exactly one whole dollar per day, plus meals. Think of that: three kroner and seventy øre, clear, each day!

I tell you these threshing machines are some wonderful things. The machine itself is driven by a large steam engine which also pulls the rig from farm to farm. Here, the grain isn't hauled into sheds before it is threshed as at home. Instead, as soon as it's cut and bound, the bundles are set up in shocks to dry. When the grain is dry the bundles are hauled together and put up into great huge stacks; generally four such stacks are set up together and the machine is put in between. Then four men stand there, each with his pitch fork, and throw the bundles into the machine. It goes like lightning I tell you! Last week we worked here on this farm, and in less than three-quarters of a day threshed about eight hundred bushels of oats. That is about two hundred barrels. The work is hard, that's for sure—everything has to go at such terrific speed.

Today I asked both my boss and the other hired man to help me get a job with a rig like this. I hope I'm lucky!

There isn't much to tell about Uncle Hans. He has worked at this same place for eleven years. He isn't nearly as rich as we imagined; no, not by a long shot. Most of the time he hasn't earned more than fourteen dollars per month; now he gets sixteen. He is also very generous; just the other day he gave ten dollars to missions. So I am quite sure he doesn't have much money. He might be worth about a thousand dollars, certainly no more, and by American standards that is sheer poverty. When I have saved up that much I will come home. Well, no, I want to have enough extra so my ticket doesn't have to come out of the thousand. In Norwegian money that will amount to three thousand, seven hundred kroner. That is real wealth, at least at home in Smeviken!

Believe me, I'm saving my money. The other day I drove a load of wheat to Clarkfield for my boss. He gave me twenty-five cents to buy dinner since I wouldn't get back until late afternoon. I took the money, thanked him nicely, and stuck it into my pocket where it still is. Do you think I could afford to spend a whole krone just for dinner? I should say not. I'd rather wait to eat until I got home. But because no one knew I hadn't eaten in town, I got nothing until supper time. By then I was good and hungry. To sit on a wagon and drive all day is no fun, you get so shaken up and empty. Still for a Nordlander who is used to going without food for twenty-four hours at a stretch, this was nothing. I only wish I could take more loads to town under those same conditions.

This will have to be enough for now. My heartiest greetings to you and Mother.

Your devoted son,
P. A. Smevik

P. S. I had sealed this letter last night but must open it again to add a few words. My boss didn't come home until long after I had gone to bed, but he had actually gotten me a job with a threshing crew. I will be leaving tomorrow afternoon and will probably be gone until around Christmas time. Since I don't know when I will be back here, I can't say when you will get the next letter. Just take it easy even if you don't hear from me before Christmas. Don't worry about me. Hurrah! Now I'll be earning some money.

Your son, *Peder*

Clarkfield, South Dakota
December 14, 1896

Dear Brother,

The first thing I did after coming home last night, tired and filthy, was to ask for mail. Sure enough, there were no less than four letters from Norway, two from Father and two from you. You could just as well have written another one, you lazy rascal, even if you had gotten only two from me. Without a word to Uncle Hans or anyone else, I flung myself down into the nearest chair and devoured the letters greedily. So you can see how much I prize news from Norway, and if you don't write often, believe me, I'll be on your neck when I get home. I have learned so many boxing and wrestling tricks now, I'm sure I can handle you easily even if you are four years older and both bigger and stronger than I am.

My heart missed a beat when I read that you almost capsized that big boat of ours out on Lidstad bay. You certainly ought to know better. You know that boat is not to be trusted without ballast; but give her plenty of weight and you can sail her as hard as you please. Your companion boat will have to reef twice, while you can go with full sail. That's been my experience. Please Andreas, you must be careful with that boat and don't go out sailing like that any more!

So Mother cried when she heard about all the trouble I had finding Uncle Hans. Poor Mother. It's perhaps best that I avoid telling things like that often; otherwise she will surely cry many times. You must be good to Mother, Andreas, and carry in wood and water for her when you are home. My conscience really hurts me when I see how considerate the men here are to the women. Sometimes I think it is a little too much of a good thing, for honestly, the women are taken care of as if they were nuggets of gold.

Of course, they should be kindly treated, but they are not exactly delicate violins either.

So there wasn't much summer herring this year. Somehow I had a feeling it would be like that. I'm sorry, but then you did have remarkably good fishing this fall as far as the coal fish and the cod are concerned. And did you really get a hundred and eighty cod in one day on the Langråsen banks? I call that a splendid catch!

Oh, how I'd like to have seen you that day as you came rowing in to Smevik bay. I bet you were as proud as King Oscar himself. But here I am gossiping about Norway and Smeviken instead of writing about America.

I must begin by telling you that I now have a nickname. Do you suppose that these porkeaters here can bring themselves to call me by my name, Peder, or Peder Andersen, or Peder Andersen Smevik? Not a chance. It's "Pete," pure and simple. If they are being extra polite it is Mister Smevik, but for every day it is as I said, just "Pete." I can't say I like it, but what can a person do? As a matter of fact, they twist all names like that. Someone who is named Ole, they call Oley; Johan becomes John. Your name in English would be Andrew. It is bad enough with the men's names, but even worse with the women's. Kari gets to be Carrie; Birgit is changed to Bella or Belle; Kjersti to Christie, and so forth. But since this seems to be the custom here in this country, there is nothing to do but get used to it.

I won't even attempt to describe how difficult the work in America has been for me. I couldn't even if I tried, and anyway it would only make Mother cry so I had better not. I would never have believed that threshing could be so strenuous. It just about killed me before I got the hang of it. I'm an old sea dog, you know, and so all farm work is new to me and much harder than if I had been used to similar work in Norway.

However, in some ways this threshing season has been both educational and interesting. Just see what a motley crew we were. There were eight men: two Irishmen, one Frenchman, one full-blooded American, one Englishman from Canada, one American-Swede (that is a Swede born in this country), one Pete, and one American-Norwegian (whose family came from the district of Voss). This Vossing was the worst of them all. I would gladly have given him a licking had there been a chance.

In my last letter to Father I tried to describe a threshing machine and how it works. I must also have told about the four men, each with a pitch fork, who do nothing but pitch bundles of grain into the machine, and believe me, that is sure plenty of work if the grain is dry and everything runs well. I was to take my place on one of the four stacks, and happened to get on the same side of the machine as the Vossing. It is the custom that once you have begun on one side of the machine, you stay there through the whole run.

This Vossing was a tall, thin fellow, lean as a fishpole. I assure you there wasn't a speck of meat on him; he was nothing but skin and bones. He wasn't especially old either, certainly not over twenty-eight. At first I was pleased to have him for my partner; after all, he was Norwegian although he scarcely ever spoke a word of Norwegian. And besides, he looked so lean and dried-up I thought it would be easy to keep up with him when we had to work at top speed. I was very soon disillusioned. Never have I seen a man who could work as hard as he could. Sometimes I even wondered if he was really human. While I stood in my shirt sleeves and worked until the sweat nearly blinded me, that Vossing—wearing a heavy jacket, a bandanna around his neck, a thick cap down over his ears, and gloves on his hands—seemed to be working just barely enough to keep himself warm. But most disgusting of all, if I am to be honest and admit the truth, he pitched three bundles into the machine to every two of mine! You know how hateful it is to be left behind so you can imagine how I came to feel toward that Vossing.

I began to hate him like the devil himself. There were other things, too, that strengthened that feeling. You know how we were brought up never to eat until we had folded our hands in prayer. I have done this as long as I can remember and I intend to continue. But I must admit that with this threshing crew it was often more than difficult. I might as well tell you (skip over this if you read the letter aloud) that there were times when I folded my hands and bowed my head and only pretended to say grace because I was too angry to pray. It just couldn't be done and that was the Vossing's fault—partly the others' too, but mostly his. He made faces and teased me in all sorts of ways. A couple of times he got the whole crowd to laugh while I was praying. I couldn't understand much of what he said as it was English. Once he told me I had better skip the introduction because with as much food as I seemed to need, I didn't have time for it. And besides, he added, the food didn't give me any more strength for all my praying, and didn't make me a better worker either! He was a light eater himself. I can assure you when he started that business about the "better worker" I got so angry it was all I could do to keep from heaving my plate right into his big mouth.

But if the Vossing didn't eat much food, he made up for it in tobacco; he not only chewed it, he devoured it. For that reason, he often ran out, although he sent for a new supply whenever there was a chance. When he was out and knew I had some, he could be as smooth as butter. He would come over and beg so nicely, "Pete, give me a chew." And I gave it to him, not because I was afraid of him; I was just glad to have some peace from his teasing for a while.

Then one night I lay awake a long time. We had worked very hard all afternoon until late into the evening, a steady grind from one o'clock until eight. When I finally got to bed my muscles ached so that I couldn't sleep. Then I began to think seriously about my situation; I began to understand that if things continued this way I couldn't hold out. My health would be ruined before the season was over. But wasn't it strange, I thought, now when it was cooler and I was certainly healthy, that I couldn't manage the work as well as the others? I knew I was just as strong as anyone; I had seen that when something was to be lifted. Therefore, it must be that I didn't know how, that I hadn't learned the trick. But I ought to be able to learn. That night I resolved that from now on I wasn't going to struggle as I had been doing, even if I lost my job. I would take it very easy and then I would observe the others, especially the Vossing. If I could only steal the art from him, I would soon show them what a greenhorn could do — especially the Vossing, that scarecrow! I was so encouraged by this bold thought that I fell asleep, and slept well too.

The next day I started to carry out my resolution and it went much better than I had expected. Every now and then I stole a glance at the Vossing and carefully noted all his movements — how he held his fork and his position each time he threw a bundle into the machine. I especially noticed how he slipped the bundle from the fork when he pitched it. It seemed to cost him no effort, while for me that was the hardest part. Often I could not get the bundle off at all, although I jerked so hard I almost fell head first off the stack. When we quit that evening, it seemed to me I had learned a great deal and was not nearly as tired as the night before. That evening I said my table prayer before supper quite boldly, without paying the slightest attention to the Vossing's teasing.

I kept this up for a week (this was the second since I started) with hard work and strict observation. Once the Vossing caught me in the act. "Now what are you staring at, kid?" Without answering, I handed him my plug of tobacco and after he had taken a large chew, I mentioned casually that he seemed to have a remarkably good grip when he handled the fork, especially when he jerked it back each time he threw. Couldn't he show me exactly how he did it? With that, I gave him the rest of the plug. Well, that was easy enough (he didn't have any tobacco of his own that day), and now in a few minutes I got all the instruction I needed. If it hadn't been for my stupid pride, I would have asked sooner and could have spared myself much sweat and still more worry about having to give up. Now things began to go better and when the run was over I wouldn't say I was the best worker in that crew, but I can safely say I was one of the best, and I was no longer afraid to compete — even with the Vossing.

Well, I ended up taking him on in another way but before I tell that story I have to tell you about one of the two Irishmen we had with us, the engineer. He was a big, fat, heavy set fellow, but kind and gentle as a lamb, at least to me, and we finally became the best of friends though I scarcely ever understood a word of what he said. At first, just after I had joined the crew, he would often come sauntering over from the engine to the stack where I worked and there he would stand and watch my ignorant struggles. Sometimes he would grab hold of me, shake his head, and make signs that I should take it easier. A couple of times he even took the fork and tried to show me how to hold it and swing it. I soon understood how sincerely he wanted to help me and became very fond of him. What made him take such great interest in me I don't know, unless it was that the Vossing tried to tease him too. Besides that, there was another thing which drew us together; we were unquestionably the biggest eaters of the crew.

When we sat down to the table, he and I made heavier raids on the platters than anyone else. Especially when we had chicken (which was often) the Irishman would attack the food like a mad man, and naturally I did my best to keep up with him. It so happened that I usually sat between the Irishman and the Vossing. When I picked up a platter, I never helped myself first as the others did, but always gave it to the Irishman. Thus I got nothing at all until the others had helped themselves to generous portions, and by then the platter was often empty. It was a hard battle for the flesh to make that sacrifice, knowing how malicious the Vossing could be. He would empty the rest of the food onto his plate, though half of it was all he needed, simply to punish me for not passing it to him first. Usually there was more in the kitchen so I got enough anyway; it was just a question of time. Yet it actually did happen a few times that I had to leave the table with a rather empty stomach.

It was my pal, the Irishman, who got me to tackle the Vossing. This is how it happened. Toward the end of the run we had several days of heavy rain, and the wheat and oats were so heavy and wet that we were constantly jamming the separator. The last day we threshed was cold and disagreeable. While the separator was being cleared we who had nothing to do thought up all kinds of tomfoolery to keep ourselves warm. Thus it happened that the Irishman shoved me against the Vossing, rather hard, too. I saw it coming and braced myself. It was worse for the Vossing; he went head first into the straw pile. Evidently this treatment did not please him, for as soon as he got to his feet again he came at me and cursed and swore that now I would get a beating.

I have never fought with anyone since I grew up, and I shall try to avoid it in the future; but now I had to defend myself as well as I could. When he swung at me with his right hand I grabbed that arm; immediately he tried to use his left, and I grabbed that one too. Thus I held both his arms. When he couldn't get them loose, he grabbed hold of mine and we began a real wrestling match. The Vossing was so angry you could see the sparks fly, but I laughed and joked the whole time for I didn't want to fight. No, he wasn't able to throw me although he tried hard enough. The problem now was how I could get away from him in a Christian manner. I had no great desire to give up and let myself be beaten, especially since the others had gathered around to watch. To talk to him was out of the question, one might as well talk to a mad bull. Finally I hit upon an idea; while we continued to twist and struggle and kick at each other, I managed to get nearer and nearer the strawpile until we were so close that we were tramping in the loose straw around the edge. I suddenly threw myself backward with all my might, put my feet into his stomach, and slung the Vossing headlong into the pile. Believe it or not, he was literally buried in the loose straw; all we saw was a pair of shoes sticking up. He was light as a feather; as I have told you before, he had no flesh on his bones. The whole crew broke out in a storm of laughter. But you should have seen the Irishman. He acted as if he were crazy; he slapped me on the back, grabbed me and danced about, all the while yelling, "Hurrah for Pete! Hurrah for Pete!" When the Vossing finally crawled out, he seemed to have had enough; he brushed himself off, took a huge chew, and sauntered away. Though I hadn't done this out of meanness or to punish him, he took it that way, and the last days the crew was together he was as nice to me as anyone could wish.

No, this will never do! My letters get much too long. I have already spent three evenings writing this one, and still I haven't told half of what I would like to. But this will have to be enough for now; I will try to write to both you and Father during Christmas. Christmas? Shucks, it looks as if it won't be very merry for me. It's not much of a holiday to poke about in the barn, milking, feeding pigs, and the like. But let's not think about that now. Hearty greetings to all!

Your affectionate brother,
P. A. Smevik

Clarkfield, South Dakota
Christmas Eve, 1896

DEAR FATHER,

We humans are certainly strange creatures, always restless, never at peace. Last year at this time we were all gathered together at home around a festive Christmas table; this year one of the family is thousands of miles away. Fortunately, none of us dreamed of such a thing then, for it would surely have put a damper on our Christmas cheer.

Many thanks for your letters, and for all the advice and admonitions. I wish they were as easy to follow as to give. You must keep in mind the saying, "When one is among wolves, one should howl like a wolf," and otherwise try to get along as best one can. Of course, I'll try not to ruin my health with overwork. I certainly don't want to come home as an invalid. Even if I should have a few thousand kroner with me, I wouldn't get any joy out of them. Life would be much simpler for me if only my nature were a little different, so that I could take things easier and not always have to do everything faster and better than anyone else. Well, we won't worry about this now, not on Christmas Eve!

You must tell Mother that she need not send me any underwear this winter. I can get along very well with what I have. Besides, winter is much shorter here than at home, and now I have bought myself an overcoat, too. I can see you wrinkle up your nose at that. However, Uncle Hans insisted that I had to have one, and even went along to town and picked it out for me. Believe me, it's a fine coat—as nice looking as any I have seen worn by rich folks at home; but it was very expensive. I paid eight dollars cash for it, about thirty kroner in Norwegian money. I was quite disgusted with myself as I drove home and thought about all the money I had spent, and figured out how much it was in Norwegian kroner. After all, you didn't pay any more than thirty-four kroner for the last boat you bought, and here I had thrown away almost as much for a piece of clothing. If that isn't aggravating to think about. When I said this to Uncle Hans, he just laughed and made fun of me. He said that if I went all winter without a coat, there would be little left of my health by spring for here the cold is really severe. As if I have never been cold before. I remember many an autumn night during the drift net fishing when I froze so that I couldn't utter a single syllable, but I never got sick from it. I told him that, too, but he said it was different in this country, and people couldn't take as much here as in Norway. That's nonsense, of course! A person can certainly stand as much cold in one place as another, unless he's a sissy. Well, the coat is bought so there is nothing more to be done about it.

I am enclosing five dollars in this letter as a Christmas present to you and Mother. I should have sent it earlier, but there was no opportunity. This will amount to eighteen or nineteen kroner; decide for yourselves what to use it for. I remember how scarce money often was during the latter part of the winter, and I am sure you can find good use for these dollars, even though they don't come in time for Christmas.

I have never before had so much money at Christmas time as this year. Think of it, fifty-one dollars. Nearly one hundred and ninety kroner! I have paid Uncle Hans thirty dollars on my ticket, so now I owe him just thirty more, and that I hope to pay him by May first. I was so unusually lucky that I managed to get a job for the winter months, and with the same man Uncle Hans is working for. I'll get ten dollars a month, which is good pay for this time of year. Most of the men work just for their board through the winter. The work is not exactly appetizing: shoveling manure, milking cows, and taking care of the pigs. Please, Father, you must keep quiet about this for if I ever come home with a little money the folks there don't need to know how I earned it.

Morning and evening when I go about my work in the barn, I can't help thinking about Andreas and the other fellows; how they are now getting their equipment ready for the Lofoten trip, and will soon be sailing northward along the channel in a driving wind, while here I am wading in cow dung! Then I feel a lump in my throat, and I often find myself speculating on how I could ever have left that life which I liked so well. I believe there is something somewhere in the Scriptures about being unfaithful to one's first love. And when I think about these things, I feel that is just what I have been. But anyway, it's good that I don't intend to stay here so very long. As soon as I've saved up one thousand dollars I'm coming home. With a little good luck that could be done in eight years. But remember I didn't promise to be home before ten years.

Whenever I tell people that I intend to go home in eight or ten years they laugh and make fun of me. Everyone assures me that I'll never see Norway again; they think that I will marry here, get a home and children, and then I'll forget Norway. Such foolish talk makes me so angry I could burst. But instead, I take my pipe, go into the kitchen, and read *Skandinaven;* and the first thing I look for is news from Norway. I think I'll subscribe to a newspaper from Norway when I have earned a little more money. Could you find out for me how much it would cost to have *Helgelands Tidende* sent to America?

It doesn't look like it will be a very happy Christmas this year. There is nothing here to enjoy oneself with. There is no public library, so no books to be borrowed; no hills, no ice for skating, only the bare prairie. The young people are going to have some Christmas dances, I guess, but I promised Mother not to dance, so I won't go to them. Besides it wouldn't be very much fun even if I did go because the young people here speak only English among themselves, so I would be left standing in a corner like the greenhorn I am. All the young people around here are Norwegian, yet strangely enough one hears them speak only English. I suppose that is so much more elegant.

The farm houses here don't lie close to each other as they do in Norway. We are four men on this place. The nearest neighbors, an old couple from Bergen, live one and a half English miles away. So you can see it isn't so easy for the young people to get together. No, there will be little pleasure for me this Christmas, except for the food, of course. But really, food isn't everything either; I've certainly found that out.

I had better close this letter now, or it will get too sad and depressing and then Mother will cry when you read it to her. So I wish you all a very merry Christmas and a happy New Year! Think of me often, and write to me even oftener.

Your devoted son,
P. A. Smevik

P.S. Just as I was about to put down my pen I remembered that I have neglected to give the four calves in the barn anything to drink this evening. So now I will have to sneak out and take care of them in the middle of this holy Christmas Eve. I can't let those poor calves suffer. Well, that's life in America.

1897

Adjusting

Clarkfield, South Dakota
February 15, 1897

DEAR BROTHER,

Your New Year's letter has long since been absorbed. I thank you for it, although you really deserve a thrashing instead. Only four pages! What kind of a brother writes only four short pages? That's almost as good as nothing, and you will certainly have to improve. Can't you understand that I have to know about absolutely every single thing? Instead of telling me about all the fun you had at Christmas this year — about skating, the Christmas parties, and all the other things you did — you let it go with only, "There wasn't much fun this Christmas." You are just as silent about other matters. About the fishing during Advent you say only, "Both the herring and other fishing were good the whole time." News like that is worse than no news at all.

If you hadn't said anything my thoughts would have had nothing to feed on and I might have been happier. I don't understand, either, how you can expect mile-long letters from me when all you write is a scant four pages. There's no justice in that.

By this time you must be at Værøy. I hope this finds you hale and hearty and in the midst of some good fishing. Greet all my friends out there.

My work this winter is rather boring. I get up at half-past six, do chores until half-past seven, then eat breakfast. If the weather is good, I haul a load of wheat to town, and get home again between four and five o'clock. Supper is at six, and then we go out and grub around in the manure again until eight. The rest of the evening is devoted to learning English.

I have gotten pretty good at English now, although I must admit that it goes more slowly than I had expected. It's a terribly difficult language to learn. The worst of it is, the words are spelled so differently from the way they are pronounced. You have to learn each word twice, both spelling and pronunciation, and that's not so easy. It's no wonder that the spelling is mixed-up for there are not as many letters in English as in Norwegian, neither æ, nor ø, nor å. Naturally that causes difficulty. The English word "honor," for instance, is pronounced "ahner" but it has to be spelled *honor*. Have you ever heard of anything so ridiculous? But I don't dare say anything about it or people will think I am dumb and don't understand anything.

There are other difficulties too. Many words sound very much alike, yet their meanings are as different as land and water. An experience I had last week will show you what I mean. I was in town one day and wanted to buy some writing supplies, pens among other items. I now know that writing materials are sold in drugstores in this country, which doesn't make sense to me. I went to the hardware store to buy a few things for my boss. While there it occurred to me that they sold steel and iron goods, and since pens are made of steel they might have some.

"Have you got any pents?" I asked.

"Pants?"

"Yes, pents."

"Yes."

Thereupon he took me through a side door into a clothing

store which belonged to the same firm, and called to one of the clerks to show me some pants. Right then I began to suspect a mistake, but didn't let on. There was a Norwegian clerk there whom I knew slightly. Very politely he asked me in Norwegian, "What kind of trousers did you want?"

"Trousers?"

"Yes, wasn't that what you wanted?"

"Ye-es, I guess I need a pair of Sunday trousers."

But of all the dozen pairs of pants he showed me I couldn't find any I liked, and of course I did not buy any either. When I got home I looked in the dictionary and found that what we use for writing are called "pens" and the other are "pants." You can see for yourself that there is a big difference in these words as far as the spelling is concerned, but I assure you that the pronunciation is so much alike that a newcomer can scarcely hear the difference. You should have heard how my boss laughed when I told him this story!

This is certainly not the only predicament I have been in on account of English. Not by a long shot. It's hard to remember some of these words, and when I forget them I'm really in trouble. One day I was in town and went into a store to buy a pair of suspenders; mine had broken in the morning as we were loading up. Uncle Hans told me before I left that the English word was "suspenders." That was such a difficult word to remember that I sat and chewed and chewed on it all the way to town, until I was absolutely certain I would remember it. And remember it I did, right until I got inside the door. But when I got up to the counter, ready to say what I wanted, wouldn't you know that word had disappeared without a trace. Was I embarrassed! There I stood, with my mouth open, staring about, unable to say a word. If it hadn't been a lady clerk, I could have explained what I wanted with gestures, but I couldn't possibly begin to point to the buttons on my pants to a lady, and a young, refined lady at that. I hurried out and was so angry I slammed the door after me. They will never see me at that store again, you can bet on that.

The worst fix I got into on account of not remembering a word was one day shortly before Christmas when I went to Clarkfield to see a doctor. That was just after I had finished the threshing run. I can't really say I was sick exactly, just felt a little poorly. I didn't have any appetite, and right after breakfast felt sick to my stomach. Uncle Hans thought it might be a touch of malaria and urged me to see a doctor. Well, one day I was feeling worse and since I was in town anyway, I decided to throw away a dollar on one of these quacks, for of course, that's what the doctors are in this country. I sauntered into the office of one of these fellows who is supposed to be able to cure anything. I knew perfectly well before I went in that the English word to use was "stomach." Isn't that a strange word? But when I got in do you suppose I could remember it? Not on your life! He was a real grouch, and I suppose I got a little flustered, so I forget. At any rate this blamed "stomach" had disappeared from my memory.

There I stood, making faces and trying to look sick, while I tried to explain in English that I had a pain below my chest, a long way below my chest. And he began to growl and scold and question me, but it all went so furiously fast that I couldn't follow. Besides he looked so angry that I was on the point of running out. But then I got angry too. Here I had been in America four months and I still couldn't manage to explain such a simple thing as being sick to my stomach. Well, I thought, if I can't use words, I will just have to get along with gestures. So I began to pat my stomach, then I opened my mouth wide and stuck my hand so far into my throat that the tears came, all the while stammering, "In the morning, in the morning." Well, that helped. The old sourpuss had to laugh at last, although I couldn't see what was so funny myself. Then he sat down and wrote a prescription for me. For this he charged me a whole dollar. Yes sir, one whole dollar. Then he told me to go to the drugstore and get the medicine.

When I came out on the street again I began to consider this, and came to the conclusion that I had better be careful. Suppose that old grouch of a doctor had misunderstood me, though I thought I had explained very clearly, and given me a medicine for some sickness I didn't have at all? Guess what I did then. I stuffed that prescription into my pocket and drove home. I told Uncle Hans that I had seen the doctor but that he hadn't given me any medicine, which was true. I should just eat eggs for breakfast, he'd said. "Well," answered Uncle Hans, "if you don't need anything more than eggs for breakfast, I'll see that you soon get well." Since then I have lived like a king on eggs. Now I'm almost tired of them, and my stomach is certainly not any worse. So now you see the many trials and tribulations of learning English.

I can't write any more this time. Please be a real good fellow and write me a long letter. You must tell me everything from Værøy, about the fishing and everything else. Is there night school this year? Who is the teacher? If it's the same one as last year, you must greet him from me. Have they gotten any new books in the fisherman's library?

Remember to write about everything.

Your affectionate brother,
P. A. Smevik

Clarkfield, South Dakota
April 28, 1897

Dear Father,

It's now more than a month since I wrote to Andreas, in fact, nearly two; and I haven't written to you since Christmas Eve. Well you have only yourselves to blame; had you written oftener, you would have received more letters in return, and that's that. Anyway, that foolishness I started out with — to write every week or every other week — why that would make thirty to forty letters a year; considering how long they are, that would be enough to fill many books. I've had to pay double postage on many of them, so in the long run it would be a big expense. Anyway there is less to write about as time goes on because I have described everything in such great detail already. And there is nothing out here but flat plains and fields, and myriads of milk cows and pigs. After a while one gets tired of writing about them.

America is certainly an odd country. Today is the twenty-eighth of April and we're almost finished with the spring work. We've planted all the barley, wheat, and oats already. Corn planting doesn't begin until about the middle of May. And now there are days as hot as you have in the middle of July. It was really amazing to see the change from winter to spring, or rather the change from winter to summer, for it's really summer already. The whole business happened in a couple of weeks. In the middle of March we had full winter with at least two feet of snow on the prairie; then came warm sunshine and mild weather and in a fortnight summer was upon us. This may sound like a fairy tale to you, but it's the truth just the same. Let me say right here that I shall never exaggerate in the least, but tell you the plain truth. If any American comes home and tells you anything that contradicts what I write in my letters, you know what you can believe.

Now I have taken part in the spring work here. The other hired man left for Montana so my boss, Uncle Hans, and I are left to run the farm. I have hired out for eight months at seventeen dollars per month; that will be about a hundred and forty dollars or four hundred kroner, which is pretty good money. You better keep quiet about this. When I come home again with a little change in my pockets I don't want to have to pay it all out in taxes!

But I was going to tell you about the spring work. It surely wasn't easy for me. I have worked with three and four horses at a time all the while, and you can imagine this was not so simple for me who had never driven even one horse until I came here. One ought to start with the ABCs in everything. However, here we don't plow with just one horse — oh no, no puttering around with anything like that; we hitch four horses to the plow at one time. And then we don't walk behind the plow, we sit up on it. The plow has an iron seat, and if you think it's too hard to sit on, which it undeniably is, you just take a cushion along! When the field has been plowed, we go over it again with another device, ten to twelve feet long and made up of large steel disks that turn. Each disk is as sharp as a sheath knife. This machine is pulled by four horses, and a man sits up on it and drives. It's used to make the soil really fine. In English the machine is called a "pulverisor," at least that's what they call it here. I doubt I have spelled it correctly, but I just don't feel like getting the dictionary; it doesn't matter anyway, if I spelled it right you probably would never be able to pronounce it.

For someone as green and dumb as I am, it's terrible to have to learn everything all at once and from the very beginning too. At the same time, I'm expected to do a full share of the work, and with the same speed and skill as an old experienced hand. No wonder I make blunders now and then. If only there were time to stop and think things over a little. But no, everything has to go with the speed of lightning. Just the same it sometimes happens that this greenhorn accomplishes something that a veteran couldn't manage.

Anyway, that's what happened last Saturday. None of the others has the slightest idea how it came about, and they're not going to find out either, but I can tell you about it. Saturday we had a forty-acre field which was to be dragged. For dragging we use three horses, hitched up side by side. We were ready to begin by eleven o'clock in the morning. The boss went out to the field with me to help me hitch up, and to show me what to do. After he had taken a few turns back and forth across the field and showed me everything, he went home, took another team, and drove to town. He didn't return until that evening after supper. I must say this dragging seemed simple and easy; all one had to do was to turn the horses at the end of the field, guide them straight down the furrow, and hurry along behind. I soon found out that it wasn't quite so easy to walk fast in that loose, pulverized soil. Even so, all went smoothly until noon. At twelve o'clock I unhitched the horses and drove them home. I put them in their stalls and fed them well with hay and oats, for I intended to work them hard that afternoon. I should have given them spikes instead of oats!

After I had rested an hour, I brought the horses out, bridled them, and started off. However, I hadn't gotten very far across the yard before I saw there must be something wrong with the bridles and the reins. The fact was that the horse that should have been on the right side I had put on the left; and the one that should have been on the left side I had put on the right, without realizing my mistake. I stopped the horses and tried to figure out what was wrong. I tried to rearrange one thing on the harness, then another, then a third. After each change, I tried to drive, but matters only got worse and worse. Finally I hit upon the scheme of changing the reins around between two of the horses. The rein which went on the outside I put on the inside, and vice versa. This helped enough so I made it out to the field at least. You see, the outside reins are shorter than the inner ones, and when I put the horses on the wrong sides the inside reins became too short. Of course it was awfully dumb of me not to see this, but the fact is I did not. I got down to the field somehow, got the horses hitched up to the drag, and set off to work. All was fine and dandy until I had to make the first turn, then the very devil got into those horses. When I pulled on the one rein and whacked with the other, I drew the horses' heads together and they began to snort and kick up their heels as if they had suddenly gone crazy. The worst of it was that I had two young horses that we'd just broken this spring and it didn't take much to excite them. When I had finally gotten them turned around and into the furrow again to go back across the field, they did not walk — no, they ran all the way down the field at a fast clip. But you, Father, have never had to run after a drag on a hot day in the loose soil over an endless field, so you can't really appreciate what I had to go through. When I got to the other end and was going to turn again, the same thing happened, only this time the horses were even wilder.

By now I was boiling mad and thought to myself that I would just have to tire these beasts out, for if running in the loose soil was hard on me, it must surely tell on them, too. When I had gotten them properly turned, I whacked them so their backsides sang, and they went down the field so fast that I could barely keep up with them. But at the end of the furrow, I realized that this was impossible for I could never hold out until evening, so this time I tried to turn the horses by going around in front of them and pulling at their bridles. They didn't like this either, and since I couldn't see behind the horses very well I almost tipped the rig, which made the nags even more unmanageable. You can't imagine how I struggled. I was angry and so hot that the sweat poured down my back. But I couldn't possibly quit for that would be a disgrace I could never live down. There was no choice but to keep on — and keep on I did, the whole afternoon. Believe it or not, the horses were wilder the last time I turned them than the first. They were on the point of running away then. By half-past five the field was done, and I felt done for too.

I was so tired, and so sore behind, that I couldn't have walked home even if I'd been given the whole farm. But that part of my body I sit on was so sore that it was impossible to ride properly, so I lay on my stomach on the horse's back, and in this way I came riding home in state. Uncle Hans was feeding the pigs, and when he saw me in this position he became angry and bawled me out for my carelessness. Suppose the horses had been frightened, how could I ever have held them? I couldn't even bear to answer him — didn't say a word. That evening my posterior ached so that I couldn't sit on the milk stool and had to kneel to milk the cows. And it was so painful every time I moved that if I hadn't been too ashamed I would have sat right down and bawled.

When the boss came home in the evening and asked me how far I had gotten with the dragging, I told him the truth, that I had finished the field by half-past five. Then he was angry, because he thought I was making fun of him.

And then I got a little angry too, and so I said that if he didn't believe me, he'd just better go down to the field and take a look for himself. And don't you suppose that he went, although it was nearly dark and a Saturday night?

"Yes," he said when he came back, "not one in a hundred could have done that!" The pain in my behind seemed to become a little more bearable. "Oh," I replied, "that's certainly no great feat!"

And now I am so sleepy I can't keep my eyes open any longer. Please, all of you, be good and write often. Remember there are many of you to write, whereas I am only one. And if some time passes before the last one who wrote gets an answer let someone else write. After I've slaved all day in this terrible heat it's not so easy to sit down and write a letter, that's for sure.

Hearty greetings to all of you, and especially to Mother!

Your devoted son,
P. A. Smevik

Clarkfield, South Dakota
August 20, 1897

DEAR BROTHER,

"Rolls the billow broad and bright, in and out along the shore." You certainly remember, Andreas, how we used to repeat those lines on a summer night as we lay out there on the sea, rocking and swaying on the swells? Ah yes, Brother, that was surely paradise for me.

So you are angry with me for not writing more often? Never mind, Brother, your scolding has no effect anyway. And besides you wouldn't write that way if you had any inkling of the conditions I'm living under. Instead, you would write a long letter to me each week, without waiting for an answer. Every Saturday and Sunday evening, regular as clock-work you would write, even if you had not heard a word from me in months.

What is the matter with me, you ask? Everything and nothing. Most likely it is only my restless Nordland blood which gives me no peace. When I look at it sensibly, I'm convinced that this is the case, because I'm completely healthy, eat like a horse, and sleep well — after midnight, that is. Before that time the heat is so unbearable that it's impossible to get to sleep; even a deep sleeper like you wouldn't be able to do it, so you know that it must be really hot. I'm not exaggerating in the least when I say it's like an oven.

America may be the promised land, but it will be some time before I'll admit it. And if it continues to be as hard on me as it has been up to now, I'll never live long enough to admit it either. Last winter I weighed one hundred and eighty pounds; the other day when I weighed myself to see how much I had gained after all this good food I've been eating, I barely reached a hundred and forty. If this continues, there won't be much left of me when I come home again. The clothes I brought with me from Norway are all so loose that the trousers hang around my legs like a couple of skirts sewed together.

The work is terribly strenuous for a newcomer; the harvest was especially hard on me. It was back-breaking work the whole time. You know what, Brother? I have come to the conclusion that if people in Norway worked as hard as they do here, there would be far more prosperity at home than there is now. People over there do not work, they only putter.

My biggest problem however is not the hard work; I can manage that somehow. The real trouble is that I am so unhappy and dissatisfied, you see. I just go moping about among the cows and pigs, thinking, "Rolls the billow broad and bright, in and out along the shore."

I can't understand these people here, least of all the young people. I just don't seem to comprehend them. Very little, if anything, of what we in Smeviken thought was fun seems to interest the fellows here. Do you remember how we used to gather on the mountainside on Sunday afternoons and evenings and amuse ourselves? Do you remember all the stories and folktales we told, and how much fun it was? Do you remember how our songs rang out over field and forest? And all the wrestling matches? And the pranks we played? We seldom got home until towards morning, yet we were as bright as sea gulls when Mother came to wake us. There is no such life here. No, this is another world, a dead world I was on the point of saying. In the first place the climate is so heavy and oppressive that it is impossible to move about even if I have time off; all my strength and energy seem paralyzed.

I just can't understand how it has happened that the Norwegian young people here in this country and those in Norway have drifted so far apart, almost as if they were of another race. It is little comfort to me to feel that I am right and they are wrong, as long as I am alone with my views. Here on Sunday nights a few fellows get together some place and tell the most vulgar stories you can imagine, or else they have a keg of beer to guzzle, which doesn't improve the stories any. If a young man has gotten ahead a little, he'll have a horse and buggy, and with this rig, strike off somewhere to see a girl and take her out for a ride. I haven't yet seen a group of boys and girls get together on a Sunday evening for a wholesome good time. That they consider too common and old-fashioned; as if the other were so much smarter and high-toned. Have you ever heard anything so preposterous? Anyway that's the way it is in this neighborhood. I hope it's better other places because this is like starving to death.

It wouldn't be so bad if I only had some books, but do you think there is anything like a public library here? Oh no, in spite of all their wealth they don't have anything like that. The only story books in Norwegian I have so far been able to find are *Uncle Tom's Cabin*, *On Skiis Over Greenland*, and *The Life of Gjest Baardsen.* The two old folks from Bergen that I mentioned in one of my earlier letters had all three. I borrowed the books from them, and this has been my Sunday fare throughout the summer. I'm sure there are English books in the homes around here, but I can't make use of them yet; they might as well be in Turkish or Chinese for all the good they do me. I don't believe the other young folks read them much either.

Oh well, perhaps I look too much on the dark side of things just now, and conditions are really better than I see them. Let us hope so, or the Babylonian captivity will surely last too long.

I was certainly happy to hear about the good fishing you had this spring. Imagine! Each one of you earned one hundred and fifty kroner in just four weeks' time. Man, that's doing even better than here in this Land of Canaan. And now it is getting so late in the season that you will soon be having dark nights; and then—then comes the herring. Shucks! I think I'll pack up and leave. What pleasure will I get from these few dollars I'm saving when I have to work so desperately hard for them, and then be miserable and unhappy besides? "Rolls the billow broad and bright, in and out along the shore." Ah yes, the billow rolls on.

I wrote this nonsense last night. I have now reread it and see that it's just foolishness, all of it. It's not really that impossible here and I have no intention of coming home before the time set. I was just extra tired and discouraged last night, and that's why the letter sounded so gloomy. I do have some fun occasionally, though of a peculiar sort. Just listen to this: Before we began the harvest, we did the haying and that is done quite differently over here. We don't put the hay under cover when it is dry as at home, but we put it up in stacks as big as houses, sometimes even bigger. Then we haul it home in the winter whenever opportunity and weather permit. To put up the hay we use a contrivance made of wood with a large block and tackle. With this machine, called a stacker, large loads can be hauled up to the top of the stack.

Two of the neighbors and my boss each have forty acre fields of hay lying side by side out on the prairie and, as could be expected, these three men get together every summer to help one another with the haying. We would help both Paal-Ola and Old Sjur, and then they would help us in return. These three fellows are all from Stjørdal — the boss, Paal-Ola, and Old Sjur. Paal-Ola is a great big strapping fellow, very easy going but if he once gets angry he has difficulty controlling himself. Old Sjur is the very opposite: a small, thin, dried-up old man with a long, coarse, dirty-yellow beard — nothing but skin and bones, trousers and asthma. He is so hotheaded and ill-tempered, with such a rasping voice, that the first time I met him I wondered what kind of a fellow this was. My boss and Old Sjur own a stacker together, and they have always let Paal-Ola use it.

It so happens that there has been the bitterest enmity

between Old Sjur and Paal-Ola ever since they first came out to this settlement thirty years ago. This year Old Sjur had gotten it into his head that he was not going to let Paal-Ola use *his* stacker; Paal-Ola could just lift that hay up with his arms, good enough for him! Long before haying time Old Sjur had told my boss that Paal-Ola was not to use the stacker this year, and he'd better remember that. My boss paid no attention to what the old man said. When Paal-Ola was ready to put up his hay, my boss and I drove the stacker over to Paal-Ola's field and began as usual to help him put up his hay. We had just gotten started when Old Sjur came tearing out. I really couldn't say which bothered him the most, his anger or his asthma; both were bad enough. He carried a large saw under his arm with which he meant to cut the stacker in two, for Paal-Ola was not going to use his half, he would see to that. By the time he got over to where we were working, he was coughing, scolding, and spitting so fiercely that we all began to laugh. The laughter became all the louder when Paal-Ola realized why Old Sjur had come, and without further ceremony picked him up, turned him over his knee like a child who is to be punished, and spanked him—with more thunder than lightning. Paal-Ola wasn't hurting the old man, far from it. When he finally got away, Old Sjur took to his heels for home as fast as he could go.

Halfway across the field, he stopped suddenly as if struck by a new idea, then came sneaking back. The work was now in full swing and no one paid the slightest attention to the old man. I stood by the stack and hauled up, using a long double tackle and a team of horses. The loads were so big it was all the horses could do to manage them. They pulled so hard they almost lay flat on the ground.

Old Sjur stood by the stack as if he were watching us.

Not a word came out of his mouth, only an occasional coughing spell and a wheezing from his chest like the sound of air being squeezed out of an old dried-up leather bag. Suddenly, as I was getting an extra big load up, the whole thing came plummeting down and I barely escaped having my head cut off. The very devil must have gotten into Old Sjur for with a single slash of his knife he had cut the rope. Having done this, the old man dashed across the prairie with all the speed he could muster, and that was a good thing, too. Paal-Ola was absolutely furious! It was all we could do to prevent him from chasing after the old man and thrashing him. Now we were in a fine fix. Eight miles from town, so it would take nearly half a day to get a new rope, and here were forty acres of good prairie hay spread to the wind and weather. While the others were busy venting their feelings toward Old Sjur, each one giving suggestions as to what ought or ought not to be done with him, I had inspected the damage and found that a long splice would easily go through the block. Not one of the men besides me on that crew knew how to splice. I guess that's why they never thought of it. In five minutes I had repaired the damage.

Paal-Ola was so happy he embraced me and promised loud and long that I would get all the beer I could drink when we got to town. I just wish he had promised me a good book instead. The work went well the rest of the day, and we actually finished the whole field by evening. It was hard work, but fun too in a way. By being able to splice that rope I won respect—fame almost. So you see, Andreas, I have some entertainment too, even if it is of a strange sort.

Be good and write to me often. Look at how long this letter is and see if you can do as well! You can say hello to that girl who sent greetings to me in your last letter. But if you should forget, it doesn't matter. She will never be the one; I'd rather find one out here.

Now I'm going to bed.

Your affectionate brother,
P. A. Smevik

P.S. "Rolls the billow broad and bright, in and out along the shore."

Clarkfield, South Dakota
December 2, 1897

DEAR FATHER,

Heartfelt thanks for your last letter as well as for the admonitions it contained. You could nicely have omitted some of them and given me more news from Smeviken instead. Not that I can't use advice, but though it may seem strange to you, the news does me much more good. It's odd that you don't realize that the only way I have of getting any information from home is through your letters —and if I don't get it that way then I don't get it at all. In his last letter, Andreas mentioned just in passing the funeral of Olina from Berget. That gave me a shock. I didn't even know she was ailing, much less dead. I remember how often she had a good snack for me when I passed her place, tired and ravenous, on my way home from school. May God bless her richly wherever she is now.

You are casual about other news too. In your last letter you tell about the fall fishing in the same terse manner:

"Fishing this fall has been very poor, perhaps less than average, due mostly to bad weather." And that is all. This might have been all right to anyone else but a fisherman, but to report to me like that about the fall fishing in Helgeland is worse than nothing. If you hadn't said anything at all, I wouldn't have gotten to thinking about it. But now I go about wondering if the fish were on the south or the north side, if there was much herring and what kind they were, if the octopus came back this year, if you caught any salmon this fall, and so on and on, endlessly. You ought to know what things an old fisherman like me would want to hear about. I remember well how you and the others sat at home and wondered why people were so lazy about writing when they went to America. I don't think it's at all strange any longer, for if the others in Norway don't take their letter writing more seriously than you do, then they don't have anything to complain about. Enough about this for now.

It's getting along toward Christmas, so I'm sending a little gift. It won't be more than five dollars this year either, but if things get too tight for you later in the winter I will try to send a little extra.

I don't expect to have an especially happy Christmas, though it ought to be better than last year. Anyway I intend to stay right here and have decided to send to *Skandinaven's* book store for five dollars worth of books. Since I don't waste my money on anything else I ought to be able to afford this, and I must have something to pass the time with during the winter besides studying English. A young person can't just sit around doing nothing. No blessing can come from that.

I am still working hard on my English, using almost every free moment I have to practice reading. The pronunciation is coming very slowly, but little by little I'm learning the meaning of the words so that now I can follow along and understand a conversation fairly well, and can even speak a little English.

May you all have a real merry Christmas, and a happy New Year. God bless you all.

Your devoted son,
P. A. Smevik

1898 Growing Unrest

Clarkfield, South Dakota
January 28, 1898

DEAR BROTHER,

Give me your hand so I can shake it good and hard, and wish you a really happy New Year. There, that's better! Now let's sit down with our pipes and have a cozy visit together; after all, it's almost a year and a half since we saw each other.

I'll start by thanking you many times over for your last letter. See, it does help to scold now and then. You were very generous this time; no one could deny that. So Father got really angry when he read my last letter. Perhaps I was rather brash, but I can't see that I was unreasonable.

You reported lots of interesting news from home. So, Hans Olsen got married at Christmas time, and to *her*. Unexpected things do happen in this world. But you say nothing about yourself, Brother, along those lines. Do you intend to be an old bachelor like me, or are you looking around for someone? I hope you find yourself a really first-rate girl and then just go right ahead and marry her. Father and Mother are getting old now, both of them, so it would be very fitting for a younger woman to come into the house, just so she is the right sort. Don't be offended, for this is certainly well-meant. And if you should happen to come across a real fine girl—one that you don't want yourself, you understand — you might let me know about her. I haven't yet seen anyone in this country that I would care to have, although I've seen plenty of pretty girls.

This reminds me of a Christmas visit my boss and I made the other day. The Nilsens, a family from Trondheim, live about six miles away. The family consists of four members: Old Nils, the father, a widower; then the young Nilsens, first Jens, thirty-nine years old, unmarried; then his sister Kari, thirty-seven years old and still unmarried, but exceedingly willing to change her status whenever the opportunity should arise; last of all comes Hans, thirty-five years old and also unmarried, but a really fine fellow just the same. Every last one of them has fiery red hair so bright that it could almost blister your face if you got too close.

Old Nils's besetting sin is that he has to be the center of attention. One time, when the Ladies Aid met at Kari's, the old man fussed around on the barn roof the whole, blessed afternoon. He moved some of the sod and stones, took a little off here and put a little on there, and every now and then he ordered Jens to bring him this or that. Every single soul who came to the place had to notice Old Nils working away up there on the barn roof. Most of them went over to speak to him and marvel at how spry he was in spite of his great age. Then Old Nils would explain that the work had been put off for so long he simply had to get at it today, and he didn't feel any older now than he did fifteen or twenty years ago.

A real, honest-to-goodness lay preacher also lives in this neighborhood; he is a strict pietist, but a very fine and respected man. He once worked for the Nilsen boys, and can you guess what Old Nils did then? When the others went in for coffee, he dashed out to hold the horses — even though there was a hitching post right in the middle of the yard to tie them to. When they came out after lunch, there stood the old man holding the horses with one hand and reading aloud from Landstad's hymn book, which he held in the other. This is supposed to be the gospel truth. You can see that the old man is a rare case but even stranger, it seems to me, are Jens and Kari. The worst is that these two are both wild to get married, and she is even worse than he. But it doesn't look as if any one will take pity on them. That's not so surprising either; I would certainly have to be in dire straits before I would marry a woman like Kari. Uncle Hans told me that she has proposed both to him and the boss. Yes, actually proposed, and several times at that. She hasn't given up all hope I guess or she would never have invited them over. I went in Uncle Hans's place.

My, oh my, they must live extravagantly. And Kari certainly can cook; she served no less than four kinds of cake with the coffee. I tried not to overeat, but I felt heavy and dull all the next day. It was fun to watch Kari flirt with the boss, and yet, though we had so much to eat and drink, it was one of the most boring afternoons I have ever spent. It was almost impossible to find anything to talk about. Four different times we started in on Jens's pigs, and four different times we had to give up on them again. So we sat there and looked at each other, and said an occasional "yes" or "no."

I wasn't nearly so lonesome this Christmas as last year. Little by little I'm beginning to get used to conditions over here and so I feel more at home. One can get used to most anything, I guess. But how anyone can *lure* people to America is more than I can understand; I wouldn't do that for all the goods and gold in the world. The greatest joy in life lies not in saving up money. Far from it! No, Andreas, do you know what is life's greatest joy? It is to be satisfied with what you have. I have come to realize this through many wakeful nights, and I know it is true. The more I see of the drudgery here, the more I'm convinced that I am right.

This winter I'm getting twelve dollars per month, and for eight months next summer will get twenty dollars per month. That will be at least seven hundred and thirty kroner, which is not bad for a farmhand with no expenses but his clothes. It does take quite a bit for shoes and clothing — these things are terribly expensive here in this country, although I don't try to dress like a king. Happiness does not depend on fine clothes.

It is getting late now and I'm going to crawl into bed. I hope this letter finds you happy and safely arrived at Værøy. I'll send it there. Greet all those who remember me. And please, Andreas, be industrious and write me a long letter!

Your affectionate brother,
P. A. Smevik

Clarkfield, South Dakota
February 28, 1898

DEAR FATHER,

This letter gives me great difficulty; I don't know just how to approach the matter. In the first part of your last letter I got nothing but reprimands, while in the last half I could read between the lines how dissatisfied you are with me. First and foremost, let me assure you that I am exactly the same person who left Smeviken a year and a half ago. Perhaps I have become a bit more independent, and nothing could be more natural, but that is all; in every other way I am just the same. You may be right in some of your complaints—but in most of them you do me the rankest injustice. I have, for instance, never intended to be arrogant toward my parents so if you have gotten that idea it is simply that you have read more into my words than was really there. It's not so easy to remember now exactly what words I used in my last letter, but I do know that there was no lack of filial respect for father and mother. You can be sure I have never felt anything like that. It could very well be that I was annoyed with you because of the very scanty news from home in your last letter. You'll just have to put up with my annoyance, you really will, because I had good reason to be annoyed—yes, downright angry. I truly have more reason to complain about lack of fatherly concern and love than you have about lack of filial respect. There you are puttering around at home in Smeviken, with little to do all winter, yet you write less than four pages every other month. But you expect me to write every other week, and that each letter should be a whole book. That is simply unjust. But let's not quarrel about this any longer; instead let us reason thus about one another: "He did the best he could, and can't be blamed because he could do no better."

And then you want to know if your name isn't good enough for me, and why I don't use Peder Andersen which is my name. Yes, Father, your name is certainly good enough. You must not believe that it is contempt for you that made me change my name from Andersen to Smevik. Let me tell you the reason for doing so. There are lots of Andersens and Anderses in America but up till now, as far as I know, there is only one Smevik. And that has certain advantages. My mail, for example, can never get mixed up with anyone else's, which could easily happen with Andersen on it. I know of at least four families near here who have that name. In a couple of these there are seven or eight members, and that makes a great many Andersens, you see. And what does it mean that I am called Andersen? It means only that I am the son of my father. But who else would I be the son of? And who isn't the son of his father? Besides that, it means that my father's name is Anders; but since the world is full of men named Anders, that doesn't mean much. This Anders may be any Peter or Paul. He may be Norwegian, Swedish or Danish, yes, even German or English, I believe. On the other hand, if I am called Smevik all the world will know that my home — my childhood home, where the old folks live — must be Smeviken, Helgeland, Norway. As far as I know there is only one person named Smevik in the entire world, so I don't need to worry about getting my name mixed up with anyone else's. So you see, Father, it wasn't disrespect for you or the name that made me change it to Smevik, but purely practical considerations. Don't do me the injustice of believing anything else. For the sake of peace and understanding between us, I'm sending you five dollars, which you can use as tobacco money for the rest of the winter and spring. I know that money is usually scarce at this time of year.

You ask me to tell you about the church situation in this country. That is more than I can do yet as I really know very little about the church over here except that it is in continual turmoil. I know of no less than four Norwegian Lutheran synods, and how many more there might be I do not know. These four are all Norwegian, they are all Lutheran, and yet they are in constant strife with one another. I don't know what they are quarreling about except that it concerns doctrine. When I understand it better myself, I'll tell you in more detail.

It is surely true that there are fine pastors here. They

seem to be men of the people. You can't imagine how kind and obliging they are, perhaps even a little too obliging. If they had a little more backbone it might often be better. I have begun to borrow books from the pastor here. He has great shelves full, and is very willing to let me read them. I have just finished reading *The Life and Times of Hans Nielsen Hauge* by that famous Helgelander of ours, Bishop Bang. As soon as I get the opportunity, I am going over to trade it for something else. From this you can see that the pastors here are not little popes as they are in Norway. Instead it is just the opposite. The congregation is the master and the pastor the servant. It's not unheard of, I understand, for a congregation to discharge their pastor when they are tired of him; they simply tell him to pack up and leave. That's what the congregation here did to its former pastor. Still, he had a number of supporters in the congregation and now those same fellows are causing a lot of trouble. They can't think up enough bad things to say about the new pastor, although he hasn't done them the slightest harm as far as I can see. They are threatening to leave this congregation, build a new church, and call their own pastor—and all this in spite of the fact that they are only ten or twelve families. Have you ever heard of such stubborn stupidity?

A free church has disadvantages as well as a state church, you see. Even such a staunch friend of the free church as you are would soon have to admit that. But as I said, I'll try to write in more detail about conditions in the church when I know more about them.

So long now. And don't go around thinking that your Per has become an Indian Chief in such a short time.

Hearty greetings to you all!

Your devoted son,
P. A. Smevik

Clarkfield, South Dakota
April 29, 1898

DEAR BROTHER,

Take it from me, a storm is brewing. You can hear the war drums and the army bugles from farm to farm. Actually, the storm has already broken loose, for some days ago the United States declared war on Spain; we are in the midst of *war*, you understand. What if this should become a world war and Norway should be drawn into the conflict? Some of the newspapers are actually hinting that a world war may not be so unlikely. Well, the Spaniards will get the beating they deserve, you can be sure of that—and good enough for them too, the way they have been carrying on down there in Cuba. They have certainly earned a thrashing, especially now since they blew up the *Maine*. Have you ever heard of anything so dastardly? They deserve to be torn apart limb from limb, and they will be, too.

You have probably read all about this in *Helgelands Tidende* so I don't need to go into more detail. I'll only add that you needn't be surprised to hear that I'm off to war. You keep absolutely mum about this to Father and Mother. No use worrying the old folks too soon. It's not at all certain that anything will come of this, but I want to go—I really and truly want to. Maybe I could win honor and fame, who knows? American history is full of examples of poor boys who have done great deeds and won a name for themselves, and this might well happen again to a daring young man.

Yesterday I was in town, and you better believe it was lively there—everyone seemed to have gone crazy. A band was playing marches, and recruits were drilling. I felt an almost irresistible urge to join them. It would certainly be a livelier dance to send a bunch of Spaniards to Manitou's happy hunting grounds than it is to sit and pull at cow teats morning and evening. Whenever I think of it, I feel the beat of martial music in my bones.

I'm going brother! See if I don't! I want to get into the Navy, be a sailor, and get out on the ocean again. Imagine, Andreas, being able to plow the waves in an American iron-clad, on which everything is made of polished shining steel. I am also becoming more and more dissatisfied with farm life and my longing for the sea is becoming stronger and stronger. That is why this is such a wonderful opportunity for me. If only they will take me with the little English I know, for I still know very little. I can write almost nothing and reading goes very slowly, too. I would promise them to work hard because you know, it is only a question of time before I learn it.

This is all I have time for but I won't seal the letter yet in case I should add more later. Now I'm going to the schoolhouse to a political meeting. It will be about the war and volunteers will have an opportunity to enlist. It's not at all improbable that I might sign up tonight.

April 30

I'll try to finish this letter tonight. The meeting yesterday evening was very lively. Five boys from this neighborhood enlisted, three of them Norwegians. No, I wasn't one of them. I found out that the rules for getting into the Navy are fairly tough. One has to be in nearly perfect physical condition, I understand, and I'm not certain that I am. I don't know if my heart can be trusted. I've made up my mind to go to a good doctor for a thorough examination. If he says I'm all right, then I'll enlist. Don't bother trying to dissuade me because if I do go, I'll be far out at sea before your next letter reaches Clarkfield. You better not write until you hear from me again. As soon as I've been to a doctor, I'll let you know.

This must be enough for now. You better read this letter to Father and Mother after all; they have a right to know all my plans. Since there isn't anything *wrong* with this, they might just as well find out now as later. Tell Mother that I am just as safe on an American battleship as I am among a herd of crazy horses and grunting pigs. Anyway we all must die sometime; whether it happens a few years earlier or later can't make so much difference, I guess. That's the way I feel about it.

Your affectionate brother,
P. A. Smevik

Clarkfield, South Dakota
May 15, 1898

DEAR BROTHER,

Just a few words to reassure you. I won't be going to war after all — at least not until this fall, and by that time the skirmish will probably be over. I went to the doctor and got my certificate from him but when I came home and got ready to leave, my boss wouldn't let me go before my time was up. You see, I hired out to him for eight months. There I stood with a long face, terribly disappointed that I couldn't get away. Next time I write I'll tell you how all this came about.

I'm in excellent health; feel as spry as a fish but I just don't thrive here and I want to get away from the farm. I don't want to continue to be just a hired man, a slave on Sundays as well as weekdays. The life of a farmer is fine for one who owns the farm and can organize the work to suit himself, but being a hired man on a large farm is certainly nothing to brag about.

I can't bring myself to write any more this time. But please, you must be kind and repay bad with good. I am discouraged and dejected, you see.

Your affectionate brother,
P. A. Smevik

Clarkfield, South Dakota
September 2, 1898

DEAR FATHER,

No doubt you people at home are thinking all sorts of strange things about me since you haven't heard for such a long time. It's difficult to explain why I haven't written sooner. I guess the reason is that I have been so uncertain and undecided, and haven't known anything definite about my future.

In your last letter you advised me to come home this fall. No, I certainly can't come home yet. I wouldn't have much money left by the time I got to Helgeland, and besides I haven't been gone more than two years. No, the only thing for me to do is to grit my teeth and keep at it.

I mustn't forget to tell you that Uncle Hans moved away

from here in May. He has built himself a nice house on his own land where he now lives. He has some cows, chickens and a small garden, and he also has a couple of large fields that he rents out. This brings him a good income and he gets along very well. Still it must be rather lonesome for him, living alone like that, but he is a confirmed bachelor. Well, there will probably be more of them in this family.

The boss and I have run the farm alone the whole summer, and it has certainly not been easy. We haven't had anyone to do the cooking or washing, so we have had to do everything ourselves, just the two of us on this three-hundred acre farm. Of livestock we have eight horses, forty head of cattle (including thirteen milk cows which have to be milked both morning and evening), one hundred and twenty pigs, and chickens by the hundreds. I really have no idea how many of them there are. The boss is a first-rate dairyman, so we also have to churn butter and do all the other chores that go with dairying. All this we two have managed this summer, so you can just bet there hasn't been much time for nonsense.

Cooking is the worst of all. To come home from the field so tired one can scarcely drag one foot after the other, and then have to prepare a meal — well, that's just too much! Even so we are getting to be real good cooks. On rainy days we study the cookbook. While the boss studies one kind of soup recipe, I tackle another. We are both great soup eaters, and so that is what we fix the most. Besides soup, we have steak with onions, eggs, and a fearful lot of sour cream. We eat as much cream as you at home eat clabbered milk. But don't envy me, for it certainly takes more than good food to make life worth living. But as I said, we live well as far as food is concerned.

Why are we alone like this? Well, you see, the boss is getting married this fall and he doesn't want another woman in the house before the wife herself comes; it wouldn't be easy for him to get anyone to come either. Womenfolk here are peculiar creatures, at least that's what those who understand such things say. Moreover, it's been very difficult to get either male or female help this year. The boss has tried all summer to hire another man. But with no luck. And with the mess we have here, it's not likely that anyone will want to come just now.

From Andreas's last letter I see that you didn't think I was serious about all my war talk. It was certainly no joke on my part. When I first began to think about it my boss promised to release me and said he would try to get another man in my place. I knew, of course, that he had no legal right to hold me if I wanted to enlist. When I had finally decided to go, I went to a competent doctor for an examination, and got from him a statement that I was perfectly fit physically. I had heard that such a certificate was necescary before I could be accepted. That was on a Saturday.

When I got home that night and told my boss I would be leaving on Monday, he almost wept, and begged me not to leave him. If I left him now, he'd have to sell almost all his livestock, it would be impossible for him to get another man who would take care of things like I had. In fact he couldn't get along with only one man, he would have to have two! There weren't any other fellows in these parts who could work the way I did. No, I mustn't desert him, things would go all to pieces for him if I left now. He kept on arguing and begging like this. Well, you know I've been with this man ever since I came to America. He had been so kind and good-hearted towards me the whole time, I began to think that leaving was wrong. He had patiently taught me all that I know about farm work, and had generously overlooked all my many mistakes. He had paid me better wages than anyone else here in this neighborhood has gotten, even though I was only a newcomer. The little English I know he is also responsible for, and a few weeks ago he added four dollars a month to my wages, although I hadn't even hinted about a raise. It can't be right to cause trouble for someone like that. The upshot of it all was that I didn't have the heart to leave him.

It isn't just to get into the war that I want to leave. No, it isn't that. But I'm beginning to see that I can't hold out for long in this life as a hired man. It is becoming more and more impossible. Not because the work is so hard; I could stand that and not grumble too much, but I have lost all interest in this kind of work. As long as it was new it was interesting, but after I had once learned it I could keep my thoughts on it no longer. They wandered off into other worlds. Therefore I have decided to try something else. I am going to attend a Norwegian-American academy this winter—in order to learn English, if for no other reason. I will leave for school in a few months. Just send my letters here for the time being for they will be forwarded to me wherever I am.

The other day I had a near accident when a team of horses ran away with me. Fortunately, I came out of it without a scratch. I won't tell about it for it would only frighten Mother. You really don't need to worry so much about me. People don't die any oftener here than in Helgeland, as far as I can see. As for you, Father, you believe that no one dies before his appointed time anyway, so why should you be so concerned about me?

You must greet Mother from me. Greet her ever so much! God bless Mother—and you too, of course, Father.

Your loving son,
P. A. Smevik

South Dakota
December, 1898

DEAR BROTHER,

"Rolls the billow broad and bright, in and out along the shore."

Your last letter brought much news, both good and bad, and I thank you for both. But most of all I thank you for writing in such detail about everything.

So Mother hasn't been feeling well this fall, and now she's had another attack of her old heart trouble. Well, I suppose that is to be expected. When I look back it seems to me that we could have done more to spare her heart from strain. Not that we were any worse to our mother than other thoughtless boys our age; on the contrary, we must have been a good deal better. But we can't deny that Mother has shed many an unnecessary tear because of our pranks and thoughtless foolishness. At this moment I can clearly see Mother as she looked the first time I ran off to a dance. You probably remember that time too. I didn't get much pleasure from it either. And then the countless times she has stood up on the hill when the weather was stormy and the seas high and stared out to see if we wouldn't soon be coming around the point. You surely remember that night four years ago when you and I had to stay overnight on Taraholmen reef? Such things are hard on a mother's heart. And I remember well how she took the news that you had been four days and nights on a deserted skerry in Fleinvær late in January, that time you capsized on your way north to Lofoten. And when she heard about the narrow escape I had on the Værøy sea that memorable twenty-fifth of January in '93, she had to take to her bed.

Many, many other incidents pass through my mind as I sit here writing this. We have had many a narrow escape, you and I; yes, for being as young as we are, we have fought many a hard fight. Just the same, I'm afraid it was often harder on her who sat at home than on us who were in the midst of the struggle. So I beg you now, Andreas, be good to Mother while she is still with you. Don't let her take a single step that you can take in her place. Help her in every way you can. Remember you have to be kind to her for both of us. I have very little money, but I'll give you a nice Christmas present this year if you will promise to be real good to Mother.

Next evening

Hurrah, now I'm a student! Well, it's true that the Norwegian teacher said in class the other day that we aren't students, we are only pupils. In Norway one becomes a student only after going to school for seven or eight years and entering the university. Phooey on that. Then I will certainly never become a student. But in America we are called students, that cannot be disputed. Here in town we are never called anything but "the students." That is exactly the same as the Norwegian word *studentene*. Unfortunately not all English words are as easy as that one.

I won't tell you about my life here this time; I will just say that I've been here almost a month and like it very much —in fact, I have never been so satisfied since I came to America. Perhaps that means something. Who knows?

Here's what I'm studying right now: American history; English reading, spelling, and grammar; arithmetic; Norwegian; and religion. All subjects and all instruction are in English except the last two which are in Norwegian, of course. Everything is quite difficult except Norwegian and religion, especially American history and arithmetic, but that is because I know so pitifully little English as yet. I have to translate most of the history lessons into Norwegian before I can learn them, and you can readily understand what heavy going that is. Then too the lessons are very long, ten to twelve pages a day that have to be as good as memorized. Many of the arithmetic problems must also be translated before I can understand them. But everything is all terribly interesting.

Just now I'm learning to work with fractions. Good heavens, but I've learned a lot in only a few days. Now I could easily figure out your Lofoten wages. A little problem like dividing fifteen hundred kroner among a boat crew of four full-share men, one double-share man, and one half-share man would be easy as one-two-three. The trick is to change the whole business into fractions with a common denominator, then divide, then multiply, and there you have it. But that's right, you don't know what a common denominator is, and since it all depends on that, there is no need of saying more. I don't know what it's called in Norwegian; anyway you would scarcely understand it even then, as it's quite complicated. You can ask Father if he remembers it from normal school.

English grammar is lots of fun and easy as water running downhill. As a matter of fact, I've won fame in that subject, and it all happened in such an amusing way that I'll have to tell you about it.

My main purpose in coming to school was first and foremost to learn English. I'll say nothing about any other dreams I may have had. Even though I hadn't the slightest idea of what getting an education involved, I did understand that it would be impossible to learn English correctly without studying English grammar.

When I enrolled here at school I mentioned this to the principal, in all modesty, naturally. He said it was no use for me to start studying grammar now, for the class already had a twelve-week head start (school started in September); also since I had no knowledge of Norwegian grammar and it was still difficult for me to read English, it would be impossible for me to begin at the beginning and catch up with the class. And of course I had to begin at the beginning.

Well, I could do nothing but accept his decision, but I wasn't satisfied. I was as industrious as an ant, and worked on the other subjects and tried to learn my lessons as well as possible. After the first week I decided I could do a little more; I felt I wasn't getting my money's worth. So I went down to the principal's office one evening—I was on my best behavior, and exceedingly diplomatic. I impressed on him that I had to have more for my hard-earned money. He asked what there was that I could take. Was there some other subject for which I had the necessary preparation? I didn't exactly know, I answered, but gradually I worked the conversation around to English grammar. I asked if I might buy a book and begin to study a little on my own. Perhaps I could ask the other boys questions if I needed help, and so get a start that way. Why, of course. He was willing to sell me a book, you may be sure, and even offered to help me in the evenings if I would come to his office. The principal is an unusually helpful and obliging man.

That was Wednesday evening. Thursday morning I had classes, so I didn't get time to look at my new book until Thursday afternoon. But then I went to work. My roommate is a kind boy and is more than willing to help me. He is much younger than I am, and I guess he thinks it's fun to teach someone who is so much bigger and older.

All Thursday afternoon I sat with the grammar, until supper at six o'clock. From seven to ten o'clock I prepared my other lessons, but from ten to twelve I had another tussle with the grammar. By that time the words were dancing before my eyes, so I crawled into bed. Friday afternoon was spent the same way. Saturday too, except that since I had no other lessons to prepare for the next day, the grammar got at least nine hours. Sunday morning I wondered a little whether to go to church or not, and debated the question while I enjoyed my morning pipe. As I sat there my thoughts wandered to your letter, and to Mother, and the meditations ended with my going to church.

As soon as I had come back and eaten my dinner, I took hold again, and again the grammar got nine hours. Monday morning I was up and at that grammar before daybreak. But when dinner finally came around I was sick and tired of the whole thing. I seemed to *smell* English grammar wherever I turned. Still, by the time I had eaten dinner and enjoyed an extra large pipe, the smell disappeared and things began to look brighter.

Then I took my book and wandered down to the principal's office. Had I come to get some help? Yes, no, not exactly. I should like to recite a little, if he had time to hear me. Had I learned something already? Oh yes. That is, I thought I knew a little. And so he took the book. How far had I gotten? About forty-four pages. At that he gave me a strange look as if he thought I was telling a lie. That made me so angry I was boiling inside. Here I had worked like a slave at that grammar and not allowed myself to rest either day or night, and this fellow took me for a liar when I wanted to show him the fruits of my labor. Then I suggested that if he didn't believe me he could just ask questions; if he wished, I could manage at least ten pages more than I first said. I had actually learned nearly sixty pages, but in the last ten there were some snarls that I hadn't quite straightened out yet, so I told him only the pages I was absolutely sure of. Then he began the questioning. I understood very well that he meant no good and intended to run me aground in a one-two-three. Maybe it was the fear of that which made my thick head as clear as a summer day; believe it or not, I saw every word clearly, up one page and down the next, lesson after lesson. Yes, it went lively as a dance. Gradually his voice became milder and he was kinder and more helpful, although I didn't need much help. I went through the whole sixty pages without stopping, and when we finally finished he looked at me strangely for a long time. Then he laughed quietly and said, "Tomorrow you may go into the class with the others. Not one in a hundred could have done this." He really didn't mean that last, but don't you think it made me feel good just the same.

And now I've been in the grammar class with the others for a whole week. How is it going? Up and down, down and up, but mostly up. I'm still hanging on, and this boy expects to stick with it, too. I have even promised myself that I'll be at the head of the class. Yes, sir.

From now until June first it will cost me about one hundred dollars—three hundred and seventy kroner! It may seem foolish to throw away that much money, but I have to try this anyway. I don't see how I can learn decent English any other way; that's why I'm here. And if I want to do something more worthwhile than pulling at cow teats all my life, then I say let the money go.

I hope things are going well for you, Andreas. A very merry Christmas and a happy New Year to you. Write as soon as you get to Lofoten so I don't have to worry all winter that something might have gone wrong on your way north.

Your "little" brother,
P. A. Smevik

1899 Struggling

South Dakota
May 23, 1899

DEAR FATHER,

Thank you for your last letter. It was good to know that Andreas reached Lofoten safe and sound. May he also have good fishing. Your letter hurt me, Father. I was both angry and depressed after reading it. I have tried to believe that you mean well and that it is only out of concern that you write the way you do. You seem to have forgotten that I am now twenty-three years old and, according to the laws of nature, ought to be able to stand on my own two feet. Since I can't expect to hold your hand all my life, I think it is about time we began to cut loose. If it should happen that the boy isn't able to walk yet, then he'll have to crawl; there is no other way. You mustn't think this is said out of disrespect for you, because it isn't. I haven't forgotten that you are my father, either. But there is one drawback to all this which you don't seem to have noticed, and that is that I live in one half of the world and you in the other. Furthermore, you are not especially well acquainted in my part of the world. Therefore I cannot understand how you can sit there at home in Smeviken and advise me as to what I should do out here on the Dakota prairie, for there is a considerable difference, let me tell you, between the two places.

I really think you carry on too much about that "throwing away your money by going to school." As if I haven't done it with the best of intentions. Furthermore, "The Lord has not given you the ability," you say. Well, you may be right, but when did He tell you that? I know perfectly well that I haven't as good a head on my shoulders as you or Andreas; I heard it often enough when I was growing up, so that's one lesson I won't forget. And "what one can't have it's no use worrying about" said the tramp in the fairy tale as he made soup from a nail. But let me ask you in all sincerity: What makes you so certain that I am no good at books? You no doubt remember how hard it was for me to memorize the catechism and the explanation. Oh yes, I remember that too. I was always an impossible dunce when it came to learning anything by heart, but I had the advantage when it came to interpretation; then I often answered when the rest of the class was stumped. Besides, that business about rote learning is the poorest argument you could find. Just the other day in Norwegian class I heard that both Bjørnstjerne Bjørnson and Jonas Lie were terrible dumbbells in school—yes, real dunces—but just see what fine men those fellows became. They both became famous. Who knows if I might not also have a talent for studying? Yes, who knows? Not that I am so presumptuous as to believe I'll ever reach the heights those men did, but suppose I managed to climb up a little higher than to be a mere fisherman in Smeviken, or a farmer on the Dakota prairie? Wouldn't these measly dollars have been well spent? I'm only asking, you understand. You think that it is ridiculous for me to waste my money on these things, but—you see—if the goal is great, the effort must be equally great. There's no getting around it, that's the way it always is. I have begun now, and I will continue as long as God grants me health and strength.

Believe it or not, I have already learned a great deal in

the five months I've been here at school. If I came home now, I would be able to get you stuck so fast that you wouldn't be able to get anywhere at all against me.

Dear Father, don't be angry with me for what I've written in this letter. It is neither arrogance nor pride, but simply that which is right and true. Remember that there comes a time in a young man's life when he has to think and act for himself. And that time has now come for me; I can't see it any other way. May the merciful God be my guide. Otherwise I'll run both boat and the cargo aground.

Greet everybody from me, both at home and away. Greet all that ask about me—and you can just as well tell them that your son Per has become a student—that is, if you are not ashamed of it.

Your respectful son,
P. A. Smevik

P.S. School is out in eight days, so send my letters to Clarkfield. I'll write to Andreas soon, I think.

P.A.S.

Clarkfield, South Dakota
September 4, 1899

MY DEAR BLESSED BROTHER,

Sometimes I doubt that I can ever become an American; I've written about this before. The last few weeks I've had another period of doubt, and this time the attack has been worse than any time before. Every once in a while these spells come over me. What is the matter? I wish I knew. I have health and strength, a good appetite, and plenty to eat. Back home in Smeviken we would call that being well-off.

Yes, you have good reason to scold me this time. I ought to have writttten long ago. It's a shame to treat such a kind, good-hearted fellow as you this way. But I didn't get your last letter before the end of June and since then I have been homeless and a wanderer on earth, with little time and even less opportunity to write a letter to Norway. Now I'll get started, and this will be a long one, too.

Heartfelt thanks for your letter, for all you told me about the Lofoten fishing, the conditions at home—for everything. You are a good brother! Kindhearted, with courage and manliness enough for two, and a better seaman I've never known to sail the channel north. But that's enough bragging for this time; next time you'll likely get a scolding. Yes, very likely you will.

I was sorry to hear that the fishing last winter failed completely. How about it, Andreas? What if you were to do what I did? No, I won't urge you to come to America; but here we have food, at least, even though we must work hard for it. Since I got your last letter I've thought about this often. Mother and Father would have to come too, of course; it would be a sin and disgrace to leave the folks alone there to fend for themselves in their old age. Think it over. If you want to come, there will be some way to get your tickets. If you sell everything, you'll have almost enough, and if it is still too little, I will try to scrape together some extra money. We could rent a farm then and take up the occupation of Cain. Not that I want to be a farmer, but you and I could help each other run the farm. I would work with you through the spring, summer, and fall; when winter came, I would take my share of the earnings and head off to school. What you must consider carefully is this: can you tear yourself away from the sea? Would you be happy working on the land all your life? You are too old to start out in the direction I have now taken. You better talk this over with the folks. I will not advise you to come for there is a good deal of selfishness in this thought of mine; in fact, I'm sure that is what brought the idea to my mind. I would like very much to have you all so near that I could see you now and then.

Now I'll tell a little about myself, as usual—a rich theme, is it not? When school closed this spring my entire treasury consisted of only seventy dollars. The problem was how to earn a lot of money during summer vacation, and since vacation lasts only three months that would take witchcraft. Farm work would bring twenty dollars a month, sixty dollars for the whole vacation, but one hundred and thirty dollars would be barely enough for my school expenses considering tuition, room and board, books, clothes, laundry, and a few cents for pocket money. Besides I didn't want to be completely broke when school closed the next spring.

There was nothing else to do but find something better paying than farm work. But what should that be? Well, after speculating long and hard, I decided to do what many another naive lad has tried: I became a book agent and went out to sell books. I had only one book, however—Heggtveit's *History of the Church*. First I went around for two weeks and took orders, then I sent for the books and made the rounds to deliver them. Then I went out after orders again. What a struggle! Of all the ways the Yankee has devised to earn money, this is by far the worst, for I can't imagine anything more thoroughly devilish. Its deception lies in that it looks so very simple, as if it were all fun and games, and filling your pockets with dollars. Well, doesn't it sound that way?

The people here are well-off, and they are enlightened;

therefore they must read and so they must buy books, that is as clear as daylight. And since everyone here is so busy and has so little opportunity to shop for books, and since I haven't seen any abundance of them hereabouts, it would be doing folks a favor to go around selling books. People ought to receive me with open arms, and even give me a few cents more than the book costs as a sort of reward. So, I reasoned, if you want to do real missionary work among the people and at the same time fill your pockets with money, then just go out and peddle books. Yes, doesn't that sound logical?

A large Norwegian settlement lies quite near the school. For many miles around, you find only Norwegians and they are well-to-do too, you understand. I decided to set my course for that settlement and with Heggtveit's *History of the Church* rake in a couple hundred dollars during the summer—at least that much.

This settlement had another advantage, too; it was so near I didn't have to throw away any money on a train ticket, but could reach it easily in one afternoon by using the apostle's horses. For the most part, however, walking is too slow going in this country.

Just as the last of my classmates headed joyfully for the railroad station to go home to friends and relatives, I set out along the country road. Long and bleak and dark it stretched out before me, full of things unknown. The songs and laughter of my friends didn't make my heart any lighter. Thoughts, those miserable thoughts, came creeping over me and I began drawing comparisons between those who were on their way home and me. Why should they be so happy—and I? They were going home to father and mother, sister and brother—and I? They could enjoy a happy, carefree vacation—and I? They didn't need to waste a single thought on the money for the next school year—but

I? No, this would never do. I did the only sensible thing, I gritted my teeth and walked on so fast the sweat poured down my back. I had to walk off this foolishness.

It was broiling hot and dusty, with not a breath of air stirring. The heat had sunk down over the prairie where it now lay and spread itself out. After an hour of strenuous walking my knees began to shake and my head grew dizzy. This was too much! I sat down by the side of the road to catch my breath, and forced myself to think about the two hundred dollars that I would soon be earning. Well, that helped. Suddenly everything seemed both lighter and brighter. I saw great heaps of gleaming silver dollars glittering and glinting before me in the afternoon sun. Of course I shall succeed. After all, I had already begun—and beginning is often the hardest part. After I got out into the country, there would be nothing to do but rake the money in. Oh yes, I would succeed, no doubt about that. When I finally started off again, the Dakota prairie seemed rather pretty.

I planned to call on a pastor that evening, hoping to get him to recommend the book for me, and perhaps put me up for the night as well. I had heard he was supposed to be a kind fellow, and that he was, too. He gave me both the recommendation and accommodation for the night. Even though I arrived there after supper was over, the pastor's wife, with her very own hands, fixed a good meal for me. I didn't dare eat as much as I really wanted to, though I was terribly hungry. You see, I had tramped nearly fourteen miles (that's two Norwegian miles, you know) since two o'clock and that brings out the appetite of a twenty-three-year-old. Well, I ate enough so that I was sure to survive until morning. The friendly pastor sat and chatted with me the whole time. He didn't have much faith in this book business of mine. His doubts didn't disturb me much, however; I was too happy about all that good food on the table.

Before I close I must tell you about the strangely beautiful memory I have from that night. It was an unusually still and pretty moonlit summer night. My room faced the church which was just across the yard. After I had opened the window and pulled the curtains aside and crept into bed, I lay awake for a long time and looked out at the church steeple. The base of the spire was white and very beautiful in the strong moonlight. With this view before me, I fell asleep. I don't know what brought it about, but that night I dreamt so beautifully of Mother. I saw her and talked with her in my sleep.

Now I can't write any more this evening—maybe I will finish the letter tomorrow night.

September 5

The next morning I got up early. It was a dull, gray everyday kind of day. A thick mist lay over the prairie, with a cold, drizzling rain. All the better, I thought. Since it's raining, today I'll find people at home. By evening I will have made twenty dollars at least. Certainly no less than that. Even if I sold only seventeen books I would earn that much. And selling seventeen books on a rainy day when folks are home, to wealthy people, educated people, people who read, people who therefore must buy books—that would be an easy matter. If I were smart and used my tongue and legs well, it might even be possible to double that. Think of it. Forty dollars in one day. I repeat—a hundred and forty-eight kroner! I dug into that blessed breakfast the pastor's wife had prepared with the courage and appetite of a young whale. Then I shook hands and thanked the pastor and his wife from the depths of my heart for their kindness to me, and when I left the house I resolved I would send her a nice Christmas present "from a stranger to whom you have been most kind." If I earned up to three hundred dollars in three months time I could afford that easily.

It had, as I said, rained during the night. The roads were all mud and slop, so I took to the edge of the road, but here the grass was so high that I was soon wet halfway up to my hips and I had to get back on the road after all. My shoes were well-worn, with holes in a few places, so it wasn't long before I heard "slurp, slurp, slurp" with every step I took.

I hurried in to the first place I came to; I wasn't bashful because I knew there were only Norwegians around here. "Is the man of the house at home?" I asked a bit nervously. "Yes, he's out feeding the pigs." I went out to find him. Over by the barn a middle-aged man was puttering about. I greeted him as respectfully and nicely as I could; I wanted to make a good impression. "Could I sell you a book, sir?" "A book? What kind of a book have you got there?" He was certainly not angry or anything. With that, I began confidently and cheerfully to explain that this was a church history, and a very good book too. Here he could see the recommendation from the pastor. "Let me see the book." "Yes, of course!" And while he paged through it, I explained that it was available in three different bindings. Finally I showed him where he should sign his name on the order blank. "No, I have no use for a book about preachers; I know those fellows so well that I don't need to read about them." With that, he walked away from me without any more discussion. I stood there awhile, completely taken aback, but then I finally realized that there was no use here for any church history. Well, I comforted myself, you could hardly expect to sell to the first man you met.

The husband was not at home at the next place, but the wife was in the kitchen washing the breakfast dishes. It was all the same to me; if the man was not at home I could just as well sell to mother, maybe even better. Boldy, I went over to her and showed her my book, and explained with great tact about the three bindings, half-leather for $2.50, leather for $3.00, and half-morocco for $3.50. She could take whichever she liked, it was all the same to me, though I would advise her, yes, urge her to take the one for three-fifty. It looked so much better, and was so much stronger that it would really be the cheapest in the long run. I talked fast and convincingly. Every now and then I noticed that she wanted to say something, but I just hurried on all the faster. I wanted to get out all my arguments this time. At last I had to stop. The woman's reply was short and curt. "We don't have time to read books." Now that was an argument I hadn't thought of. I laughed and tried to turn the whole thing into a joke. She never said a word. "All right, missus, I will put you down for one at three-fifty, or do you prefer the one at three dollars?" I must say I didn't like those eyes of hers when she turned and looked at me. "I said we don't have time to read books here in this house." This was spoken so sharply that I almost jumped. She grabbed the broom and began to sweep until the dust was thick in the room. I understood then that there would be no sale here either, so I put on my hat and sneaked off.

This was beginning to look somewhat strange. Here I had been working for two hours straight and still hadn't sold a single book. I tramped doggedly on, in spite of the slurping in my shoes. At the next farm three men were sitting on the barn doorsill, smoking their pipes. As I saw them sitting there so comfortably, a happy thought came to me: here I will surely be able to sell three books at once. I explained my errand and showed them the book. I gave it to the man nearest me. He immediately handed it over to the next one, who didn't open it either, but gave it to the third man with these words: "You better buy the book,

Ola!" Can you guess what Ola did then? Well, he set it up on a stone against the barn wall, then leisurely filled his pipe, all the time asking me all kinds of questions: where I came from, how long I had gone to school, what I was studying, if I could do farm work, and so forth. And when he had gotten all the answers, he wanted to know if I would hire out to him for twenty dollars a month! No, I didn't think so, at least not yet, but couldn't I sell him a book? A book? No, he had a house full of books, he could sell me loads of them, but as he said, if I wanted honest work, then—. The other two men had long ago sneaked away. And since it appeared just as impossible to sell Ola a church history as to go to the moon, I had to leave this place also without success.

My steps were not so confident when I left that farm and started down the road again. The truth was that I was completely discouraged—completely! If things continued this way it would be slim pickings. There wouldn't be any three hundred dollars, nor any Christmas present for the pastor's wife. Nevertheless, I plodded on; but at the next farm I came to, my luck was no better either. Here I met the stubbornest old coot from Trondheim that I have ever come across. The worst of it was that he made such a fool of me. First he looked through the book very thoroughly—don't you suppose he even read long passages? Then he laid the book carefully aside, as if he only wanted to decide which binding he should have before giving me the order. I waited expectantly and finally began to talk favorably about the binding at $3.50. It would look so good in the book case. And it could be passed on to the children, to the grandchildren, and even to their children too. The man said nothing for awhile. Then he began to talk about something else entirely. He wanted to know what school I came from. "Hm. Is that so?" And did I know that teacher? And that one? And that one, too? "So-o-o. What kind of fellows are they?" Then I began to brag about the teachers and I became really eloquent, which was natural enough for they had all treated me just like a son, and given me both advice and help. I said what was true, that the school was undoubtedly the best school in America, and that no better teachers could be found anywhere—about this there could be only one opinion. When I had finally talked myself dry, he sneered spitefully, and then he began to tell me what kind of fellows the teachers were and what kind of a school it was, and what kind of a fellow I was, who was ashamed of honest work, and chased around the country trying to palm off such foolishness on folks. I have never heard so much evil come out of one man's mouth in so short a time. Sparks fairly sizzled around him!

I knew, when I had recovered from the shock, that here there was no use for any church history. But then my temper flared. And you may remember, Andreas, that when that happens I don't usually have to search for words. He spoke his Trondheim dialect and I my Helgeland dialect, and words flew back and forth. It ended when he rose and swore that he would throw me out. Then I shouted that if he had the courage, if he dared to come down to the road, I would beat him up so thoroughly that his wife would have to search high and low to find all the pieces. Of course that wasn't a nice thing to say, and not worthy of a student; but, by golly, these were extraordinary circumstances. Anyhow that half hour with the Trondheimer was a stormy debate all the way. Later I found out that a nephew of his had been kicked out of our school a couple of years ago because of bad behavior. That was the reason for the uncle's great fervor.

When I came to the next farm I was still so angry that I didn't care two hoots whether I sold a book or not. I went in anyway, and found a kind, pleasant and God-fearing old widow. And here the miracle happened. I sold a book. It's true, it was one for only $2.50. As I lay awake during the night and thought about the day's troubles, I realized the widow had bought the book out of sheer sympathy for me.

Well, if I were to tell all that happened to me and all my troubles that day it would be too much for me to write and for you to read, so I won't. I will only mention that I had no dinner that day, that I sold one book for $3.50 in the late afternoon, and that I was lucky enough to find a good-hearted family to stay overnight with. But never have I been as sore in body and spirit as when I turned in that night.

I kept on with this business exactly one month. Then I figured enough was enough. In that month I had made twenty-five dollars. No more, no less. Since then I've been wandering around, sometimes working by the day, other times by the job. I've done almost anything you can name —dug wells, helped build windmills, butchered hogs, picked corn, and so forth. It hasn't always been fun and games either, that you must realize. Yet these things are nothing compared to being a book agent. So far, I have scrounged together one hundred and five dollars. I intend to continue picking corn until some time in November, so I can earn another sixty dollars. Then off to school again. The worst of it is that I'll miss the first ten weeks, since school begins around the sixteenth of September. That can't be helped. I will just have to clamp down hard with studying at night and try to catch up with the boys.

This certainly got to be a long letter. A hearty "so long" for this time—and if you ever come to America, never try your luck as a book agent!

Your brother,
P. A. Smevik

1900

Fulfillment

South Dakota
February 18, 1900

DEAR FATHER,

It's been a long time since you last heard from me. I am well, fit as a fiddle, and everything is fine, except that I'm so terribly sleepy. I think I could sleep for two whole months and not be completely rested. Even thinking of it makes me yawn. This drowsiness comes from too much studying at night.

I came to school two months late this fall because I had to scrape together as much money as possible first. In all my classes the others had a head start and, since I had to begin at the beginning with everything, it was really a struggle to catch up. It was hardest to catch up in Latin and algebra. Latin is difficult, but very interesting. Yes sir, I actually can read Latin and can already write such simple sentences as "Via est longa" (The road is long), "Vir filio dat consilium" (The man gives his son advice), "Nauta vento et remis portatur" (The sailor is carried by wind and oars), "Labor omnia vincit" (Labor conquers all). And whatever you may say about my abilities I can answer this: either most of the pupils at the school are impossibly dumb or else your son Per has a good head after all; I certainly catch on just as easily as the best of these fellows. No, this is not bragging. But it was harder to catch up in algebra than in

Latin. Anyway that is a very difficult subject, a sort of arithmetic where letters are used instead of numbers. The unknown quantity, the number one is searching for, is represented by a letter. And then one tries to find the sum that the letter stands for. It is too complicated to explain in a letter, but if I could talk to you I would try to show you how it is done. I am now studying this subject in all my free time, and hope to catch up with the class by the end of the year.

This term I am studying the following subjects: Latin, algebra, world history, American literature and world literature, geography, physics, Norwegian and religion. Everything is interesting, but the best of all are world history, physics, and Norwegian. Yes, I like religion too. I like everything! In spite of the fact that my courses are more difficult this year than last, and that I have more of them, too, things are going better. There are two reasons for this: I am beginning to get a much better understanding of these things, and I understand English so much better. It doesn't happen so often anymore that I come to an English word I can't guess the meaning of. That much, at least, I have learned since I started school.

This fall I was fortunate enough to get a job here at the academy. I work for my board, and since that is the biggest expense, I will manage nicely as far as money is concerned. My wallet won't be nearly so thin this spring as it was last year. It certainly isn't any refined work I have. The boys jokingly call me the chimney sweep. The work consists of emptying the ashes out of the school stoves, carrying in coal every evening, and sweeping the floors. But I'm not fussy about the lack of gentility; I'm used to a little of everything, I, the fisherboy from Nordland; besides I do this work in the evening after all the others have gone to bed.

As you can see, I am enjoying the life here. Yes, I like

it very much; I'm like a fish swimming in roily water. What pleases me most is that everything is so democratic—among both teachers and students. Here I am—the fisherboy, newcomer, and greenhorn who understands nothing—yet I'm equal to the pastor's son and all the other sons in the world. You find no other differences in rank here except that which comes of talents or a good mind. The one who is lucky enough to be gifted is looked up to with the greatest respect. Certainly there are a few snobs among us who try to make something of themselves with fine clothes and such, but they are exceptions. We also have our literary societies with debates where we sometimes tear loose until fur flies. All in all, this is a cheerful and lively life—a little too lively to suit me.

Most of the students are kind and good-hearted, smart, quick-witted, and clever. There are a few dumbbells who ought to be in a blacksmith shop swinging a sledge hammer, rather than being students and poring over books. That is very clearly seen and more clearly heard. The other day in Norwegian class, for instance, one of these sons of wisdom couldn't get it through his thick head that a guardian angel was not an angel who could shoot, since the words for "guardian" and "shoot" are very similar in Norwegian. During assemblies when I look out over the student body, it seems to me there is a lack of leadership material; there are few princes here.

Certainly there are things I don't like; that is to be expected in all walks of life. The greatest fault is that the young people are so finicky and complain about the food at the school, which I think is a sin and a shame. For breakfast we get good oatmeal with all the sweet milk and sugar we want. Besides that we get the most delicious fresh wheat bread, butter, and coffee. I can see how your mouth waters at the thought of such a breakfast. For dinner we have fresh meat and potatoes with bread and butter, as much as we are able to eat. Isn't that a fine meal? For supper we have bread and butter, syrup, sauce, and coffee. I think this is real good fare — I don't know any better — and you can bet I fill up too. But don't you suppose most of them turn up their noses and talk as if they'll get tuberculosis and die from the food? This has often disgusted me. They should have had thin gruel and sour herring for every meal — the way I can remember we had for two winters when I was a small boy. Then they would change their tune. The strangest of all is that many talk as if they had better meals at home, but I have visited hundreds of families in South Dakota and seldom have I found as good food as we get here at school.

There are other things I don't like about the students but it's not easy to explain what they are. It's something I feel rather than understand. Do you remember that old pauper, Fiddler Joe, there at home a few years ago? He seemed to understand fiddles very well and said often that the violin had to have a good *sounding board* or it was no good. The tone depended on this. I'm not so sure I understand what he meant by his philosophizing about the sounding board, but it seems to me sometimes that this is what is wrong with these young people. Their sounding boards must be too thick or too uneven or else they aren't made of the right material. Our Norwegian teacher gets spells sometimes when he talks inspiringly about "enthusiasm for the high ideals of life." I am far from certain that I understand this, but I do understand clearly that for most of the class this kind of talk is like throwing water over a duck's back. The sounding board doesn't give any response; there must be something wrong with it. That deep irresistible yearning which every wholesome young person ought to have toward an ideal is lacking. As I said, I don't understand these things so very well myself, so it's possible that I may be doing the boys an injustice.

I have forgotten to thank you for the letter. I thank you now. I'm just skipping over your reprimand. After I sent my last letter I buried the tomahawk, and I don't intend to go and dig it up again. I have set out on a path that I intend to follow as long as there is a spark of life in me, in spite of anything you might have against it. And so, period. It's foolish for you and me who haven't exchanged an unfriendly word in twenty years to begin to quarrel now when we each live in our own half of the world, and are father and son besides.

God bless you all. Greet Mother with a thousand greetings.

Your devoted son,
P. A. Smevik

South Dakota
September 18, 1900

DEAR ANDREAS,

"Rolls the billow . . ."

Whew, how you scold! The worst of it is I deserve every bit of it, and more besides. Of course I have excuses, but I don't want to trot them out. A man who comes with excuses when he has neglected to do his simple duty, it seems to me, is like one who stammers and stutters and can't get a word out when he is to give an important command. It is always so embarrassing to listen to. Therefore I humbly bend my back and you can whack away. There is just one thing I want to say in this connection which is not meant as an excuse, but rather an explanation. After one has lived in this country a few years, the letters to Norway will inevitably become fewer and farther apart. Little by little, as a man gets a foothold here, he gets acquainted and acquires friends; he gets a home, and a person like me even gets many of them in many different places. He associates with these friends and acquaintances, in person and by letter, until they become a part of his life. And quite unnoticed Norway and the life he lived there will become locked up in a separate room in his soul. This room is a kind of holy temple which he enters only now and then as is fitting and proper with anything sacred. The more selfish he is the less often he visits his shrine, because each time he goes there his heart becomes so strangely heavy and lonely. And as there are very few who enjoy being in that state of mind, therefore . . . . Yes, I deserve the whipping, so fire away.

Thank you anyway for your letter; not just one, but a thousand thanks. It's sad to hear that Mother is failing steadily. You know what, Andreas? I sometimes have a premonition that I may never get to see her again. God grant that it's only a bad dream. However it is very uncertain whether or not I will ever set foot on Norwegian soil again. That foolish talk of mine when I left home about returning in ten years is nothing to count on. It's impossible to promise such a thing for so far into the future. If I am to reach the goals I have set myself — and I believe that with God's help I will — then it is perhaps best that I remain on this side of the Atlantic. It would probably be difficult for one who is educated over here to get a position in Norway; the good people over there seem to believe that everything that comes from America is just humbug — which shows more clearly than anything else how unpardonably ignorant those same good people are.

So, you think you'd like to come to America but you don't want to desert the folks, and they won't leave? It is just as well you feel this way and also that they feel the way they do. It would be comparatively easy for you to go back if you don't like the life here (that is, of course, if you didn't stay too long), but for them to return would be pretty nearly impossible.

I have just returned to school. This year I'm going to go the whole year. How wonderful that will be; imagine being able to keep at my books for nine months in a row.

This summer I did something entirely different. I had tried so many things before, none of which seemed to suit me, so I thought to myself, "You better try something else, Per." And that I did. I taught parochial school! I had many pupils, yet everything went unexpectedly well. One thing is certain though, my heart was in my throat the first day and it took a long time before I got it down to where it belongs, but I put on my most serious expression and jumped in. It was no wonder my knees shook, for I remembered so clearly how as a thirteen-year-old I helped revolt against the teacher, and how we boys from that day on had the reins in our own hands. Yet we weren't more than thirty, counting both boys and girls, while here I had fifty of them. I didn't have much trouble keeping control of the flock. The children behaved as children usually do, not any better and not very much worse. Teaching school is by far the most interesting work I have tried, although it isn't nearly as easy as I thought when I, myself, struggled away at Luther's Explanation. I lay awake many nights and pondered how this or that point could be made clear, or how this or that little scamp could be reached. It is certainly not as easy as you may think. Far from it. Imagine that you had a catechism class of ten- or eleven-year-olds and you had to explain the first, sixth, ninth, and tenth commandments. How would you clear that hurdle? How would you make these truths understandable to children of that age, make them so simple that they could be grasped and held fast for life? It is a little more difficult than you imagine.

On the whole the school was rather successful. But there was something else which gave me many gray hairs before my time, even though they haven't shown up yet. The congregation had no pastor; the one they had called was not coming until fall. Just as I was closing school on Wednesday of the first week, I was visited by the church council. I couldn't imagine what this meant and became very flustered. I thought perhaps they had come to fire me. It could easily be that I had said or done something — inexperienced as I was — that wasn't according to their cookbook. After a short, and for me painful, conversation about the weather, crops, the school and the children, they finally came out with their errand. They wanted me to conduct church services every other Sunday while I was there! Conduct services? Me? Yes, or devotions. The congregation gathered in the church every other Sunday for the morning service, and then someone read a sermon. But I had, after all, been to school and was a student and therefore I could preach to them, yes, that I could. I tell you, Andreas, I didn't know what I should do. I could have sunk through the floor. I tried my best to convince them that having been to school a couple of years didn't mean that a man was prepared to preach and interpret God's word. But it was no use. They wouldn't listen. They kept on arguing and trying to convince me. I had to, they said, and all the time I knew I simply couldn't. Well then, if I felt that I absolutely couldn't preach, then I could read a sermon for them; for I, who had gone to school ought to be able to read much better than any of them. Besides, I could decide later. All they asked at this time was that I take charge of the meeting the following Sunday, and they knew I wouldn't refuse that. With this expression of trust and confidence, they went their way.

That evening and throughout the night I was in great distress, and groaned in misery. Me preach? Me give a sermon? I could read a sermon, certainly I could do that. But the congregation was expecting me to preach. They all expected it. They could read a sermon themselves. I wasn't as much of a man as they had thought; the teacher they had gotten this year didn't amount to much; here he came straight from school, and still he couldn't preach for half an hour for their edification. That's what every mother's son of them would think. How provoking.

There wasn't much rest for me that night. Thursday, I did my work at school in a half daze. When classes were finally over and the last curly head had disappeared, I sat down at my desk and prayed to God for help in my hour of need. Then I looked up the text for the following Sunday, which happened to be the story of Peter's miraculous draft of fish. Wasn't this strange, that it should be that particular text? The draft of fish as a text for the fisherman's first sermon? It occurred to me at once that if there was any text in the Bible I could preach about, it was this one. Then I began to study the story and all its details, and as sure as I'm sitting here writing to you, I saw the whole situation before me as large as life. I saw the sea, I saw the tired fishermen lying there on the shore after the night's struggle with their nets, I saw the Savior come down to them in the morning light, I heard his conversation with the exhausted men, and I saw the miracle that followed. Clearest of all, I saw the Savior and Peter; I seemed actually to hear the earnestness in that memorable conversation that followed between them. Then I began to write my first sermon. It got to be about the confession of sin, and the Savior's infinite love and readiness to forgive. That night I wrote until late and likewise Friday night too, and when I finally crawled into bed on Saturday night, I had something ready that might be called a talk; considered as a sermon, it was certainly an example of everything it should not be. Yet the worst came on Sunday morning when I was to get up and preach. I hope no one will ever feel his own unworthiness more than I, at that moment, felt mine. At first my knees shook so I could scarcely stand; but when I heard the sound of my own voice I gradually gained confidence, and the whole thing went unexpectedly well. I don't mean to imply that I preached so well, it only seemed to me that it went well. I preached four Sundays. How much good my listeners got out of it, I do not know, but I do know that I, myself, benefited greatly. I learned more in some respects, and grew stronger spiritually through these weeks than I perhaps had done through my entire previous life. Yes, Brother, America is a strange land, that's for sure. You can never guess today what you may run across tomorrow.

September 19

When I began this letter I didn't intend to write about myself but the thoughts came that way, so I scribbled them down. I meant to write a little about conditions in the church among the immigrants, something both you and Father have asked about in almost every letter. The worst of it is, I am not at all certain I can get everything right. I haven't been here long enough yet to fully understand this free church, nor have I been around much to the various congregations, so I can't say I'm familiar with the facts. Besides, there are so many Norwegian Lutheran synods over here, and I am personally acquainted with only one of them. But by putting together what I've seen with my own eyes and what I've read in the newspapers, I can come to some conclusions. Whatever else may be said of the church, I am positively certain of one thing: it is the church that has saved the immigrants from going straight to the dogs. Many of our countrymen over here have developed into nothing but dried-up runts. Others are, and will remain, caterpillars; the butterfly spirit has been destroyed in some way or other. But this is certain: there would have been much more trash and wasted human potential if it hadn't been for the church. Yes, of that there is not the slightest doubt.

It is impossible for one who hasn't seen it to imagine how the church has followed in the footsteps of the pioneer — followed him through struggle and suffering into the wilderness, into the forest, and out over the endless prairie; how the church, like a mother, has taken him by the hand, asked him to straighten his back, rest a moment and look upward. The back was straightened, the head became more erect too, and the eye received visions of glory from above. For the early pioneers, there was no force other than the church which could draw mind and thought away from the struggle for survival. It is miraculous how it has been able to open the hearts of the people. Truly, it is a hard battle for flesh and blood to give and give and give again — and then to borrow money so as to have something to give — when one has labored so hard to scrape together a few pennies. It is enough to make one's own selfish nature burn and smart in agony. I remember that agony well from my first year over here when a persistent old man from Bergen begged and pleaded, pleaded and begged, until he persuaded me to donate two dollars to the congregation.

However, it isn't all bright and glorious within the Norwegian Lutheran Church here either. Ever since the early '80s, there has been a storm of dissension hanging over it, and this storm has sometimes raged so hard that it has threatened to tear the whole house to pieces. How hateful and uncharitable some people can become when they begin in earnest to argue about the true faith. At times one is tempted to doubt that they will ever become citizens of the Kingdom of Heaven.

Where I was this summer there were two congregations on account of such a disagreement. The original congregation had been split apart by the battle. The people in both congregations had helped build the original church. After the split a very difficult question arose: which of these two groups had the right to the building? To share the church by using it on alternate Sundays, for example, would never do. Certainly not. Both congregations claimed the right to it, so they took it to court — the only matter on which they agreed. After a couple years of squabbling and lawsuits and heavy expenses on both sides, one of the congregations was awarded the church, and the other had to get out. By then the hatred was well-nourished, you might know; it ate into the very marrow of the people; and the whole community became like a huge, festering boil full of all kinds of malice and ugliness. Folks who had formerly lived side by side as good neighbors now looked at one another with hatred and mistrust, and caused each other as much trouble as possible while still keeping within the law. Not only were the congregation and the community split and broken up but worse still, even families were torn apart. It's the brutal truth that father opposed son and son opposed father, and that brother fought his brother. I recall two brothers out there, both of them old men. The one was chairman of the council in his congregation; the other held the same office in the other congregation. People swore it was true that these brothers hadn't greeted each other in twelve years although they lived in the same neighborhood and often met in town and on the road. What do you think of that, Andreas?

Now let me tell you about a little incident concerning one of these brothers. It shows very clearly what people will do when hatred has worked its acid through their whole being. When I went out there, it seemed to me there were too few pupils at school the first days. I asked if these were all the children in the neighborhood. "No, far from it! But the others won't send their children to school because they think you are teaching false doctrine." This explanation made me both depressed and angry. So one evening I borrowed a bicycle and rode around and talked to people about sending their children to school. I explained to them as nicely as I could that I had been confirmed in Norway and that I wouldn't give any interpretation other than the one I had from there. Besides that, I would try to teach the children to read and write a little Norwegian, and they would be perfectly safe from any kind of wrong teachings on my part. Well, that helped beyond all expectations. I got many tousleheads that way.

Now it has always been my weakness, you know, to have to play the fence-mender; I always have to tinker with anything that is out of order. This, I suppose, was the reason that in an unguarded moment I conceived the poetic notion that since I was so successful in getting the children together, why not try it with the adults too? In my youthful enthusiasm, I really thought it could be done. To that end I formulated a very simple but rather ingenious plan: We would have a picnic on the last day of school; I planned to prepare a program consisting of readings and songs by the children; then I would give a talk, myself. As the main attraction the report cards would be given out and each child would receive a beautifully decorated souvenir card; the grades would be read to the whole gathering. Everyone in the neighborhood would be invited to the festivities. The more I thought about the plan the happier I was with it; it developed into a kind of passion with me. So one Sunday after our devotional service, I stood up and laid the matter before the congregation, although I kept quiet about my real purpose. Well, the people weren't unwilling, and a committee was elected on the spot to take care of everything except the program. Monday afternoon, before closing school, I brought up the matter there. I asked the youngsters what they thought about a picnic on the last day of school. "Oh, that would be lots of fun!" And when I suggested we might also have some games after the program, such as "last couple out" and "prisoner's base," their eyes fairly sparkled. Whereupon it was solemnly decreed that we were to have the school picnic.

The weeks that followed were very busy ones. The regular work had to be pushed as hard as possible; I still had to prepare my sermon every other Sunday, and now an extra speech for this program; and I also had to find small pieces and songs for the children which had to be learned and practiced. But the work went like play for I enjoyed it. Not only did I enjoy the work, but I was secretly happy over the prospect of getting those old fighting cocks to celebrate together. Perhaps this would help melt the ice that lay around their hearts.

Well, here is what happened. When the rival congregation heard about the program the teacher was arranging, there were both misgivings and doubts. The question now became: could they, would it be right for them to participate in this festivity with their bitter enemies? Just how their philosophizing worked is difficult to say. Anyhow the majority came to the conclusion that since this affair was for the children, it would be all right for them to attend just to see what was going on. Especially since harvest was over and they weren't so busy, yes, they would just amble over to take a look, that was all. It is certainly remarkable what drawing power there is in a mother's love, and in her pride and joy in her children.

The chairman of the church council in that other congregation was quite a psychologist. Without a doubt he had smelled a rat and guessed what my intentions were. He also understood there was danger afoot, and that those confounded youngsters could easily lead the older folks into temptation and sin. While he brooded about this, he had a brilliant idea, which convinced me of his deep insight into human nature. No, Andreas, you could never guess what this brilliant idea was; you are too good-hearted. It takes one who is really permeated with hatred and evil to conceive such a plot. Yes, this honorable *pater* (*pater* is Latin for father) in the church council went to town and brought home two kegs of beer. Then he invited the men in his congregation — for the Sunday I was to have the school picnic and at exactly the same time of day — to come out to his farm and gulp down all the beer they could hold. After he had extended these invitations, he got another brilliant idea, and it was the best yet: he went to town and bought another keg of beer and then he sent out an invitation to the men in our congregation, too. That wasn't so dumb for a sixty-year-old. I've seen things done by wiser men that haven't been half so smart, but the old man had miscalculated on one point. He was a little too old, poor fellow, and he had forgotten what miraculous power that little curly head has over mother and father when he has really set his heart on something, and begins to beg and plead, plead and beg without stopping. It was this power that helped me, for most of the parents who had children in school came to the picnic.

The other party was rather dry and dull, I heard afterward, in spite of all the liquid they had. I am deeply ashamed to admit that our sexton wasn't strong enough to withstand temptation, although he was the only one of our people who went to that party. He partook with such good-will and brotherly love that he soon was drunk as a coot. The sexton's downfall was perhaps due to two things: in the first place he was a Swede, and in the second place, he had no child with a chubby little dirty hand to lead him on the straight and narrow path. Here you have an example of what zeal for the pure faith can lead to.

Speaking of sextons, I might as well tell you about the sexton's family in the other congregation. This story isn't quite so sad. These sextons are surely strange fellows — at least, some of them. Well, sextons are sextons, and will be sextons forever. The family consisted of only the two: the sexton himself, named Andreas (Dear Brother, I can't help it that he has your name!) and his wife, Madam Sexton, whose name is Anna. When the strife first arose in the congregation — as luck would have it — the sexton came to see the matter from one side, while the Madam came to see it from the exact opposite. Steadily and faithfully, both night and day, he tried to convert her to his point of view, and she strove just as hard to convert him to hers.

In temperament they were both alike and unlike. He was sulky and cranky, selfish and contrary as a stubborn old mule, dishonorable in his efforts to convert her. After trying both threats and persuasion, he resorted to underhanded tricks in order to maneuver her into his fold. Anna, on the other hand, was more like a sexton should be: good-hearted and generous to the poor and needy, but stubborn and quarrelsome, and as stiff as an old broom when she had gotten an idea into her head. Life with Andreas had by no means sweetened her disposition.

After more than a year of heated debate from both sides, the truth finally dawned on them that in reality they belonged to different synods; the split in the church had also separated them. Then Andreas renewed his efforts with more zeal than ever. To be the sexton of one congregation and let his wife belong to another was a disgrace he couldn't live down. So he tried again, first with threats — but with no result, for Anna just laughed and said with icy contempt, "You just try, Andreas!" She could well afford to answer that way, for physically she was much stronger than he. Then he took to his bed, sulked and refused to eat. He wanted to die now, he said. As far as Anna was concerned that would be just fine — then there would be peace in the house at last. She let him lie there without paying the slightest attention; instead she hitched up the horse, and visited her sisters in the faith and had coffee and other good things. Then he pretended to have visions and revelations. "What do you see, then, Andreas?" "I see a church that is about to fall down." "Hm, that's your church, Andreas." The last thing he came up with was pretending to be crazy. One day as they were eating dinner — they had had an especially lively debate at breakfast that morning — Andreas suddenly began to heave the dishes at the wall, first the coffee cups, then the saucers, and then the cream pitcher. He didn't get any further than that in his berserk rage. For when the cream pitcher went, the Madam arose in all her dignity and power, grabbed the poker, and people swear it's the truth that she used it effectively, too. At any rate, from that day forward there has been a sort of truce in the house.

This happened more than ten years ago, but those two old folks are still acting like idiots. Andreas subscribes to one church paper; Anna to the other. She supports one congregation; he the other. When he gave twenty dollars to his church, she forced him to hand over another twenty dollars which she conscientiously gave to her church. I know this is true for Anna told me so herself. I have never seen anything so irresistibly funny as the relationship between these two. Certainly it is pathetic too, but it's not the pathetic side that strikes one first.

Now you musn't think that it is like this in all communities and in all congregations over here, for it certainly is not. This is an unusual situation. But these were the conditions where I was this summer. I have told about this in such great detail so that you and Father could see that all is not glorious in a free church either. With the insight I now have into conditions in the church over here, I really don't know which is better, a free church or a state church. The only thing I do know with certainty is that one has advantages that the other lacks, and *vice versa.*

Now that you have read this letter to the end, I think you ought to be able to forgive me for taking so long to answer yours. I really do.

Your affectionate brother,
P. A. Smevik

1901 Losses and Gains

South Dakota
March 4, 1901

DEAR GRIEF-STRICKEN FATHER,

Since I received your last letter it seems almost as though there is nothing left to live for. Life has become so unbearably empty. One busy, dull gray day is exactly like every other dull gray day. Sunshine and happiness are hidden far, far behind the clouds. It seems to me as if they will never break through again; spring and summer have disappeared forever.

After I read your letter, I put on my hat and coat and walked far out into the country to a lonely place. I had to be alone. There I sat down and read your letter one more time. And then, finally, the dam broke, and I wept like a little boy who has had a whipping. It wasn't very manly of me; but manliness would scarcely have given Mother back again. When I went home after a while, I felt as if a secret place in the innermost recesses of my heart had suddenly become locked and could never again be reopened. The worst of it was that in that inner room I had hidden everything that was beautiful and precious and worth preserving.

At times I can hardly believe that Mother is really dead. It seems so unreasonable and so completely incomprehensible. And I had built up such beautiful castles in the air about how well I would take care of you and Mother in your old age. But I suppose I had not been good and kind enough to her while we were together to be granted that joy. The good Lord doeth all things well; he has now given her a better home than any I could ever have given her. How full of sin and selfishness we mortals can be! Even though I know so well that she is much better off now than with anything I could have arranged for her, don't you suppose I am ready to rebuke God for not allowing me to keep her longer? Yes, we humans are like that.

Now, Father, please write and tell me in detail about Mother's passing. It wasn't to be expected that you could manage that so soon afterwards, but now when the worst has subsided a little, you must do that. Where does she lie in the cemetery? I remember where Grandmother and Grandfather are buried so you need only tell me how close she is to them, and on which side. Please ask someone to plant a little birch tree by the side of Mother's grave as a remembrance from me; then it can keep the watch over her that I wasn't allowed to keep. Mother would like that, for she was always so fond of the birch, especially when it unfolded its leaves in the spring.

Poor Father, it's hardest for you. Whenever I think of you all alone at home, the dull gray day becomes even duller and grayer. Don't you think it would be just as well for you to come over to me now? I have no home of my own yet, but that will surely come in time. And one thing I promise — and you can depend on it — that as long as I live and am able to work you shall never lack for food and shelter. I certainly won't try to entice you to come to America, but I believe I can be of more comfort and help to you in your old age if you come here than if you remain in Norway. Uncle Hans still lives alone and I am sure he would be pleased to have you come to him, and you could stay there until I have a home of my own. Think it over. In the meantime I will write to Uncle Hans and Andreas and see what they think about this.

As you see, I am at school again. This is my last year here. I shall then take my final exams, and graduate (as they say here) in the spring. I can truthfully say that I have done well. I will finish in less time than anyone else before me. This is no doubt due to the fact that I have used my time with the same care as a miser uses his pieces of gold. Next fall I will try to get into a college and continue there. You see I have become convinced that if God created me for a special purpose then it is to work with books. But now there is little joy in getting ahead for she who rejoiced the most over my success, and in that way doubled my pleasure — her praise is forever stilled.

Hearty greetings to you Father. God bless you, and help you to bear your great sorrow.

Your loving son,
P. A. Smevik

South Dakota
May 15, 1901

DEAR BROTHER ANDREAS,

Hearty thanks for writing so soon. From the tone of your letter, I can hear how lonely and empty the house has become since Mother left. Well, you know that is to be expected. There is no use in complaining, for that won't bring her back, not that you complain so much; it rather seems that you say too little. It's not in the lines I read your unhappiness, but between them.

Yes, it is sad to think that she had neither one of her boys with her in her last hour; you were in Lofoten and I was here in America. I am certain that she missed us, and missed us very much. At the time of her death, I dreamt about her two nights in a row. The dream was the same both nights, except that it was much clearer the second night. It was so vivid then that I couldn't sleep any more. I got up, lit the lamp and sat down to study, but that didn't help. My thoughts turned constantly to Mother; I simply could not keep them away from her. So I got dressed and slipped quietly from my room out into the cold, moonlit winter night. There I took a long walk and let my thoughts wander undisturbed to Mother and home, and many other things far off in Norway.

What did I dream? I dreamt that I stood on the other side of Smevik bay, and on the hillside by our house I saw Mother, dressed in her Sunday best. It looked as if she was ready to go somewhere far away. She waved at me and called to me to come across the bay so she could say good-bye. The dream was so vivid that I recognized the clothes she was wearing; I heard her voice clearly. Only one thing seemed strange about the dream. Over the bay, the house, Mother, and the whole scene there lay a supernatural peace and stillness. It was because of this that I could hear her words so clearly across the distance of the bay, yet she spoke in her normal tone of voice. Wasn't it strange that I should have had that dream two nights in a row, just at that time? Can you explain it? Did she, perchance, get permission to pass by here on the way to the heavenly home to bid her son farewell? If anyone should be granted such a wish, it would have to be Mother.

So you have begun to think seriously about coming to

America? In that connection you ask many questions, some of which are rather difficult to answer. The old saying that, "One fool can ask more questions than ten wise men can answer," again shows itself to be true. Now you know that no offense was meant by this remark. You ask me to explain what you eventually would gain by coming to America. That is much easier said than done. Why don't you turn the question around and ask what you would lose? The latter I can probably answer more easily than the former. I am still too much of a newcomer to be able to discuss with any justice all the advantages this country has to offer the immigrant. It is possible that the answer I give now would not be the same twenty or forty years hence; nor do I know how my children, grandchildren and great-grandchildren will come to see the matter. What advantages will they have because I came to America? I ought to know all these things in order to give you a fair answer. Just now I had a brilliant idea. Last year at a Fourth of July celebration (Fourth of July is America's Seventeenth of May) I heard a speech on the theme: "What is gained and what is lost, upon exchanging the Fatherland for the new land." I have a copy of this speech. For the most part I am in complete agreement with it, and since the speech answers your questions much better than I can, I will send you some excerpts from it. You must read them with due consideration. Please let Father read them too.

"We who are assembled here today for this occasion are adopted children, that is, the majority of us are. We have sprung from a different root, and have come from another people. Hence, this festive day cannot have the same significance for us that it will have for our descendants. Even though we are foreign children, we wish to help celebrate this country's national holiday. It is our right and our duty. It is our right because the adopted child belongs to the family and has the same rights as the natural child. It is our duty to celebrate the Fourth of July because we ought to show our new mother honor on her birthday. But let us honor her in a worthy manner, brothers. Let our homage be such that she will understand more clearly that noble blood flows in the veins of the children she took to herself from the Northland — and let us prove to her that her family has been enriched by much good human material.

We are adopted children. Let us today dwell a little on that truth, for it is a solemn truth and we do well to remind ourselves of it often. America is our country, but not our Fatherland. When the ship bearing us or our parents sailed westward into the unknown, when Norway's gray coast with its snow covered peaks sank into the sea, then our Fatherland sank with it. As such it exists for us no more. When we came here and received our citizenship papers and became Americans, we swore obedience and allegiance to the United States of America; but at the same time we forswore all our citizen's rights in that impoverished land we had left behind — in truth a serious oath! Thus were we adopted. Thus you and I exchanged our Fatherland for a new land.

And now in this festive hour, I think that you and I ought to try to come to a clearer understanding of what was gained and what was lost in this exchange. It is time that we immigrants come to some conclusion about this, if we haven't already done so.

Broadly speaking we can certainly say that much was lost, but also that much was received in return. Quoting the poet we may say:

> "Stort har jeg mistet, men stort jeg fik,
> Bedst var det kan hende, det gik som det gik,
> Og saa faar du ha tak da Gud."

"Much have I lost, but much I received,
Perhaps it was best that it happened this way,
Thank you then, O God."

Yes, truly there has been much won and much lost. There are large figures on both sides of the balance sheet. If I were to ask any of you at this very moment which was the greater — the loss or the gain — most of you would doubtless reply the gain, and that may very well be correct. You have beautiful, well kept farms here. You have built fine houses. Undeniably most of you have done well. There is wealth in the Norwegian settlements of the northwest today, no doubt about that. But these things have certainly not come of themselves; you have not gotten them for nothing; you have had to struggle hard and suffer much need before you got to where you now stand. Let us pause a moment and consider what these things have cost. You have experienced all the struggles and privations that the pioneer life had to offer. Thirty or forty years ago it wasn't so easy for a poor family to come here. In the old country you had a home, at least most of you did. Although that home was ever so poor and humble, it was possible with work and frugality to live there. This home you abandoned and came to a strange continent. But, the promised land was no paradise; there was no shortage of land, but it was wild and the wilderness had to be cleared. A hole was dug in the hillside. This dug-out became the home where you lived both summer and winter. Then the land was cleared and plowed but it went slowly — so terribly slowly — for there were no tools, no horses, only two bare hands to do all the work, and how unspeakably tired they often became. The family increased; there were new mouths crying for food, more bodies to clothe. You worked early and late to keep body and soul together, and to retain the land on which you had settled. This is but a small portion of what your present wealth has cost you.

But why bring out all these dark memories? Let us also recall the brighter ones, for it was not all toil and suffering and poverty. From the long years of hardship, you have reaped rich blessings; God has in full measure rewarded your labors. Success came slowly, but it came; the small fields grew bit by bit; one piece of machinery was acquired, then another, then several. The oxen were traded for horses. The dugout was replaced by a shanty. Thus things have improved little by little until now — yes, what do we see now? The shanties have disappeared. Instead there are magnificent houses and farm buildings of all kinds. It can be said in all truthfulness that you have become wealthy. And this prosperity is the first thing I will mention as a gain in your exchange of your Fatherland for this new country. It cannot be denied that many of you could have become prosperous in Norway, too, if you had expended as much energy and labor with as much ambition and enterprise as you have done since you came here.

Right here, in connection with this idea, I want to mention another benefit which you have received in this exchange: the practical grasp of things that you were forced to adopt when you came here. Also, you were forced to pay attention to time. Here you soon realized that the old saying, "Time is money," is more than just talk. No matter how dearly we love our friends and relatives over there, we have to admit that the great majority of them do not understand the value of really economical intensive work. The way they waste and fritter away time! Neither is that enterprising spirit — that shrewd, progressive, food-producing ambition — so well developed in them. Or have you forgotten how you never saw any other way of doing the work than the methods your father and grandfather and forefathers for generations had used? If you had done things the same way here, there would have been hard times and starvation in this country, too.

Let us consider a few more of the advantages you received in the exchange. There is the great personal growth you experienced by coming to a new land, and mingling with foreign people. It is very fruitful to blend one's own ideas with those of strangers. By this process you received new thoughts which unconsciously became a part of yourselves. Your outlook was broadened, and you developed more than you realized. This was a hard school as we shall later see, but it was a good school. And easy or difficult, it was an unavoidable necessity in order to survive over here.

The fourth benefit we received when we exchanged our Fatherland for this new country was the great freedom which we enjoy here, both civil and religious. From a purely theoretical point of view, Norway is more democratic than America, and yet it can be truthfully said that no human beings under the sun enjoy the same freedoms as the American farmer. His independence is almost boundless. The only masters he knows are the sun and the rain, and the tax commissioner. Anyway the taxes are so reasonable in this country that no one need complain about them. It is quite different in many European countries where taxes are so high that it is difficult for rich and poor alike to stand up under the burden.

But the greatest advantage that we received when we exchanged our Fatherland for this country is the rich variety of opportunities this land has to offer each individual. No matter how poor a young man may be, no matter how humble his ancestry, if he has the courage and the will power he can succeed. There are innumerable examples of Askeladden, the poor little ash boy, winning the princess and half the kingdom. Let us look at a few. The great railroad king, Jim Hill, began with just his bare hands and became a millionaire. John Lind, one of America's ablest politicians, emigrated to this country as a poor fourteen-year-old boy; at one time he ran a threshing machine in eastern Minnesota. And Knute Nelson, the boy from Voss who reached as high a position in government as it it possible for an immigrant to reach, was once a shepherd boy. When the Civil War broke out General Grant was earning his living by hauling cordwood. President Andrew Johnson was the son of a tailor, and he himself worked as a tailor's apprentice. And one of the greatest of all of history's great men, Abraham Lincoln, first saw the light of day in a simple log cabin in Kentucky. But why mention all these names? You will find them on nearly every page of this country's history. And if you look at this country's intellectual leaders, you will meet the same sight again. Thousands upon thousands of young men, with no other help except a pair of strong hands and an undaunted spirit, have struggled through school after school until they finally reached their longed-for goal. It is not only the Yankee boy who has accomplished this. No, it can be said without boasting, and it should be said with pride, that the lad from the foreign land — the adopted child, for whom the difficulties have been even greater — has accomplished it just as often, if not oftener, and just as well, if not better, than the native son. And these rich and varied opportunities for the individual are, in my opinion, the greatest of all the benefits we received when we exchanged our Fatherland for this country.

However, there were not just advantages to this exchange. Wealth is a great earthly benefit; an extensive civil and religious liberty is certainly a blessing; rich opportunities for each individual is one of the Creator's gifts to mankind. But life is more than food, earthly happiness is more than civic freedom, and God's greatest gift to man is not first and foremost great opportunities. When I consider all that we forfeited in this exchange, all the other things that make life worth living and that fill the years with true happiness, then I wonder at times if what we gave in exchange was not worth more than what we received. Let us turn the page now and see what we find on the other side of the ledger.

The first loss, I find, is that ennobling and uplifting influence which a mighty and magnificent nature has on the human mind. All eminent men who have studied this question agree that the natural environment exerts a great influence on us. It must be so! Why otherwise do you decorate your houses? Why otherwise do you mothers polish your kitchens every day? You cannot bear to see things disorderly and dirty. Why can't you bear this? Because it makes you depressed and discouraged. So it is with the nature that surrounds us, with this difference, perhaps, that the impressions of nature work on us more unconsciously for they remain the same day after day, year in and year out. Now you must not infer that I believe America has no natural beauty, for it certainly has. The West is, after all, famous in that respect. Even the prairies of the Middle West have their beauty. When we, for example, sit out on the porch on a warm midsummer evening and listen to the rustling of the half-ripened grain, when we hear how this rustling blends harmoniously with the monotonous tones of the crickets, the grasshoppers and the frogs — then the prairie is truly beautiful. There is no doubt about that. And yet this beauty is insignificant compared with that of your Fatherland. This is proven by the ever-increasing stream of tourists who visit Norway each year. There is almost unanimous agreement that nowhere else have they found such an impressive, such a sublime beauty as they find there. They could scarcely say anything else either, for all extremes of nature are found in Norway. There the brilliant summer reaches its hand to the eternal glaciers of the polar regions. And the northern summer nights! No, not night at all, but day — an enchanted fairy day. Time and time again artists have tried to capture on canvas that blending of light and color which the northern summer night spreads over land and sea, but to no avail. The traveler will find mountain peaks as wild as any in Switzerland. He will find mountain chains so majestic that they compare favorably with the Alps; fjords, of which the Scots have seen no equal; and beyond these, he can find valleys whose charm reminds him of Italy. Over the entire landscape lie the deep organ tones of the rivers and the waterfalls. Then there is the sea — so powerful, so melancholy, so awe-inspiring in its anger, and so bewitching in its calmness. There are folks from Western Norway in this gathering, I see. They know how true this is. I remember so well my first weeks in America, in the eastern part of Wisconsin. Near the farm where I worked were some high, wild hills. On my first Sunday there (I had had my first lesson in milking that evening) I scrambled up through the weeds and brush to the top of the highest hill. The sweat ran and the nettles burned my face, but I went on nevertheless. When I finally reached the top, I stood completely still and stared out and out; my eye wandered over the entire horizon as I searched and hunted in vain for the sea. I am not ashamed to say that as I walked home that night I was not far from tears. This one incident shows in a way what power the Norwegian nature has had upon me. And I, for my part, believe it to be an indisputable fact that the reason Norway has produced so many artists in various fields can be attributed largely to her magnificent nature. The prairie has not yet produced any really great artist.

This loss that I have mentioned, great as it is, is a small

thing compared with another: We lost our Fatherland — the bitterest, the heaviest, the most irreparable loss of all. To lose one's Fatherland — exactly what is meant by that? Ah, brothers, that is more than you and I can bear to speak about today. Anyway, I am sure you know what it means. Or have you forgotten that parting so many, many years ago? Don't you remember how unspeakably difficult it was? Oh yes, you remember it well. One doesn't easily forget his farewell to family and friends, and the last handclasp with his gray-haired father and mother. And when the cottage on the hill and the church spire disappeared from view, and your eyes became misty, then a strange heaviness fell upon your heart. This is not to be wondered at for then the most tender and sensitive heart strings snapped. These things are not easily forgotten. They usually remain in one's memory as long as one lives. The Norwegians are a very warm-hearted people, it is said, and for this reason they feel such a loss very keenly.

Giving up our Fatherland means more than getting a wound that can never be healed in this life. It also means that we have forfeited spiritual contact with our own people and our own nation. And that, brothers, is a very severe loss. It is difficult to live among a strange people, a people with a completely different outlook on life than our own. It is painful to always feel that you are a stranger among strangers. You've never felt that, you say? No that isn't to be expected out here in these large Norwegian settlements where everything is nearly the same as you were accustomed to in the old country. But how many thousands and thousands are there in our large cities who have experienced this, do you suppose? How many fine Norwegians have landed in an insane asylum for just this reason? All that coldness, strangeness, and homesickness — that sick, hurting, gnawing longing — drove them finally into madness, either that or into vice. For there were times when the longing for home and family had to be deadened, and so it was deadened in the dives of the big city. This has happened to many a fine Norwegian youth. But even though it hasn't always gone quite so badly — and thank God it doesn't — yet this feeling of forever being a stranger is an unpleasant companion. It follows one as faithfully as a shadow. Even in the midst of happiness, it may come forth and cast its darkness over everything. This feeling of being an alien causes a discordant note even in the most joyful laughter.

These that we have mentioned here are cruel losses, irreparably cruel. But if we had lost no more than this, there would be little reason to complain, especially when we remember what we won. Let us take a closer look at the balance sheet.

When we severed our ties with our Fatherland, we became not only strangers among strangers, but we were cut off from our own nation and became strangers to our own people. Our pulse no longer throbs in rhythm with the hearts of our own kindred. We have become strangers; strangers to those we left, and strangers to those we came to. The Fatherland to which we had centuries of inherited rights, we have given away, and we of the first generation can never get another. Let me repeat: We have become outsiders to the people we left, and we are also outsiders among the people to whom we came. Thus we have ceased to be a harmonious part of a greater whole; we have become something apart, something torn loose, without any organic connections either here in America or over in Norway. Our souls can no longer burn with genuine national enthusiasm. That uplifting and ennobling of the spirit which every true citizen experiences in a national crisis can never be felt by us. In short, we have become rootless. One of our most important nerves has been cut. We are alienated. This speech is perhaps unclear to some of you. Let me, therefore, ask a question or two: Have you ever felt that you are a real American? Do you feel that the American people are really your people? A small, a very small percentage of Norwegian-Americans seem to feel that way but I doubt that they really do, deep down in their hearts. This I know, most of us do not; we are simply unable to. As a result, we can never enter into the public life of this country to the degree that our education and intelligence give us the unquestionable right to. Well then, suppose we sold out and went back to Norway to live. Would we not feel at home then, we who are so Norwegian in all respects? No, herein lies the greatest tragedy of all. We would feel like strangers there too. For a few, it seems to work out, but for the great majority who try, it proves unsuccessful. They believed themselves to be Norwegians, but soon discovered they were not. Here they had acquired attitudes, unconsciously perhaps, that didn't fit into the conditions they found over there. First, they tried to become Americans, but found they couldn't; then they wanted to become Norwegians again, but found that to be equally impossible. Herein lies the tragedy of emigration. If you give up your Fatherland for good, it can never be regained; neither can you get another in its place, no matter what you do.

Whenever I think these thoughts, tragic as they are, I am reminded of an anecdote from Østerdal that the Norwegian writer J. B. Bull tells. There was a gypsy who traveled about between the villages there. The man's name was Mikkel. He was handy and clever as most gypsies are, and since he could do just about anything people asked him, he was nicknamed Tinker Mikkel. Once he came to a pastor's farm where there were many children, as is fitting and proper. At this farm they had a music box, but it played only one tune — a waltz. Every now and then one of the children would go over and wind it up. The pastor's wife finally became sick and tired of this continual waltz, so she asked Mikkel one day as he strolled into the farm if he couldn't take the waltz tune out and put in a hymn instead. Yes, Tinker Mikkel would try, so he took the music box and disappeared for a week. "Well, how did it go?" asked the wife, when Mikkel returned with the box. "Did you get the hymn tune in?" Tinker Mikkel scratched his head as he replied, "Well, I don't really know. I got the hymn in, but it was harder to get the waltz out." When they wound up the box and let it play, out came the strangest music they had ever heard. It was a hymn melody in waltz time. Now and then came snatches of the hymn, then a bit of the waltz, then both hymn and waltz together. Thus it is with us foreign born here in this country: we are neither the one nor the other, we are both at the same time.

And still we haven't accounted for everything in the ledger. No, there are some figures left so large we can scarcely comprehend them. And if we talked for days on this theme, we could not tell everything. The truth is this, brothers, that no one can ever fully explain what it means to lose his Fatherland. We can have a more or less clear feeling of it, but this feeling we cannot express in words. We lost the inexpressible! The saddest of all is that one never realizes these things before it is too late. If people in the Old Country could see things as you and I do, then it would not be long until that stream of emigrants would be nearly dried up . . ."

Then the speaker went on to show that the loss was greater than the gain not only for the first generation, but also for the second and the third, and that it was impossible for anyone to say definitely when this loss could be fully overcome.

But I won't copy that part of the speech. You aren't married and perhaps never will be either, so you're not particularly interested in the second and third generations. Besides I can't write any more; I have been copying this speech for two evenings now and I'm tired of it. You must read it thoughtfully. I believe what the speaker says is true. I've been thinking the same thoughts myself; perhaps this is why I liked the speech so well.

You can understand that I will not tell you to come to America. No, I won't even advise you to do it. I will just say that you need never worry about food and clothing. They just seem to come by themselves.

I had a letter from Uncle Hans some time ago; he advised me to get you and Father to come here this fall. He says that both of you can stay with him all winter, and you won't have to do a thing. He thinks it is best for you to hold an auction immediately, and come as soon as possible. Then you can avoid going to Lofoten this winter and Father won't have to be alone. This is not bad advice; if you really intend to come, the sooner the better. But let me know as soon as you have made any final decision.

In just two weeks I'm through here. It is sad to be so alone. All my classmates are now busy sending invitations to relatives and friends, and getting ready for commencement activities. I don't have anyone to invite except Uncle Hans, and he says he can't come. On the other hand, I have the honor of giving a speech at the graduation ceremony. Well, that honor doesn't mean much to me, since none of my own people can get pleasure from it.

Right after graduation I am going to North Dakota to teach parochial school. I don't know yet how long I will be there. You can send my letters to Uncle Hans, and he will forward them to me.

May God help and guide you to make the right decision about coming to America.

Your affectionate brother,
P. A. Smevik

Lewisville, North Dakota
July 29, 1901

DEAR BROTHER AND FATHER,

Your last letter, Andreas, made me both happy and sad. So you have finally decided to come. Well, I am pleased about that in a way — I only hope this decision will bring happiness for you too. But let me tell you once more before it is too late that I do not advise you to come to America.

You ask me to give you the necessary instructions for your trip which I shall do to the best of my ability. Your plan to have the auction around the fifteenth of next month, and leave September seventh is quite all right, I am sure. And since you expect to get enough money, it will not be necessary for me to send you any. That's just as well, since my wallet is rather thin right now. You can buy your tickets in Trondheim. I would advise you to take the Scandinavian-American Line; that is best, I think. It goes direct to New York, and you will avoid having to go across England and can be at sea the whole time instead. Of course there are many interesting things to see in England but emigrants don't get to see much anyway, and besides you will have plenty of new things to see for a long time after you've gotten here. Buy your tickets all the way to Clarkfield, South Dakota. No, you don't need to take any food along from home, but when you arrive in New York I advise you to get some provisions for the train trip. The agent in New York (he can speak Norwegian) will help you buy them. You can count on almost three days from New York to Clarkfield.

As soon as you step ashore, you must be sure to send me a few lines and tell me when you landed. The letter will reach me before you do, and it will help me be at the station in Clarkfield at the right time. Don't worry, I will meet you at the station whether I get your letter or not. And if you don't see me at the station as soon as you get off the train, just sit down and wait until I come. I will come! As soon as I'm through teaching school up here, I'm going down to stay with Uncle Hans. And when it gets along toward the time you should be coming, I'll go to Clarkfield and stay there a few days so I can meet every single train that comes. You can count on finding me.

There should be no problem in connection with the journey as far as I can see, none whatsoever. Here is some advice which you absolutely must remember: when you are on the train be sure to show your ticket often. It isn't difficult to see who the conductor is; you can tell by his cap. Show him your ticket every now and then, for you will have to change trains two or three times, you see. When the conductor motions for you to get off the train, just go ahead and step off, you don't need to worry about getting lost. When you get into the station, show your tickets to the clerk there. That way he will know what train to send you off on, and when he signals you to step on board, obey blindly. All this is very important for you to remember. I can't think of anything else to tell you now. You will get along fine, so don't worry.

When I realize how soon I will see you, I'm so happy that I sing! This may be selfishness on my part but it can't be helped.

I have finally met someone up here who comes from our part of Nordland. She is Jensine Pedersen from Strømmen. I doubt that Andreas remembers her, but Father knew her well. She says she is distantly related to us. When she heard my name, she immediately sent me a special invitation to come for a visit, which you can be sure I accepted with pleasure. Jensine is married now and has a large family. They belong to a different congregation than I do.Up here there has been a terrible uproar between three congregations, or more correctly between three synods. But we let the church strife rest as there was too much else to talk about. She hadn't had a letter or any sort of news from home in fifteen years, and I guess she hadn't written in all that time either. So you see that there are Helgelanders a good deal worse than I am. But you musn't believe she had forgotten her childhood home. I tell you, it was marvelous to listen to her when she drew aside the curtain and began to bring the memories forth. Oh no, nothing had been forgotten. I was ashamed to find that she remembered people and events much better than I even though she had been in America thirty-five years and I only five. My goodness, how she questioned me about everything and everyone. She was simply starved for news. I talked and talked, and in return she treated me like a prince. The worst of it was that I didn't get to bed until three o'clock in the morning. She just had to hear more about Norway, and I just had to tell her. I was finally allowed to go home, but not before I had promised to come again the next evening. I will have to tell you a little about that, too. Since this will be the last letter you'll get from me before you leave Norway, I can afford to steal a few hours from my sleep and write you about it.

Well, the next evening after an excellent supper, just as I had lit my pipe and settled myself comfortably on the porch and the talk about Norway had begun to make our hearts glow, a man drove into the yard. He wanted to know if the school teacher was here. Yes? Could he please talk to him? I was rather surprised since I had never seen this man before.

He was a strange figure as he sat hunched up in the wagon —small, dirty and ragged, with long grayish-brown whiskers. On his head he wore a dark brown, round old hat with a narrow brim. His words came slowly and softly as if he were frightened and hesitant. Umm, could I come out to his farm tomorrow afternoon and conduct a funeral? *Me, conduct a funeral?* Hm, ye-es,—his little boy was dead. No, I couldn't do that. A pastor was needed. Hm, well, he couldn't get one. He had driven around all afternoon, but all the pastors were away. (He was lying, which I did not know until later.) No, I was only a teacher, and he must have a pastor to conduct a funeral service. Hm, well, he knew that I couldn't perform the graveside ceremony, but couldn't I come along to the graveyard and—and—just read the ritual—hm, well, just do that much? Now it became my turn to say "hm." In my head I heard a clear and distinct "No," but deep down in my heart I thought I could hear an even louder "Yes." The longer I looked at that man, and saw how bowed down and dejected he appeared, the stronger the voice from below became. How far was it to his home then? Twenty miles. Twenty miles! Hm, well, but he would get one of the neighbors who had some pretty fast horses to come and get me. And don't you suppose that I in my foolish lack of judgement promised to go? I will never again listen to those voices from below!

The next day at noon a fine buggy with two magnificent horses stood before the schoolhouse door. I took my Bible and hymn book and went with the driver. On the way out I began to ask about this man whose little boy was dead. Bit by bit I heard a strange story, one that was not to my liking. The man's name was Tor Sima. He was the bitterest free-thinker and blasphemer in these parts; he never went to church and, whenever and wherever an opportunity arose, he sneered at everything that was holy. He had had four children, all boys. Two of them had died only a year apart, and now when the third one passed away the other day, Tor began to think things over. Perhaps there was a God after all, and perhaps He was angry because Tor had not had the children baptized, and had not given the two a Christian burial either. Yes, that must be the way it is, thought Tor. And so, the neighbor said, Tor had decided to get someone to speak God's word over the body of this boy. Then maybe his bad luck would stop and he would be allowed to keep his fourth son. So Tor Sima had selected me to prevent further catastrophe. You can imagine how I felt when I received this information. Many times I opened my mouth to tell the man to drive me back again, but each time I kept silent and let it go.

When we got there I found a genuine pioneer farm. Tor's house was small and low and shabby, as could be expected in such conditions. Inside, the little black coffin stood in the middle of the room. The father sat at one end, the mother at the other. Poor wretched mother! She was so shattered that it was pitiful to see. I greeted them and sat down to find the hymns.Then I tried to find an appropriate text. The night before I had chosen a passage and studied some of its main points, but after the information the neighbor had given me I discarded it. I was now determined to preach the *law* to these people, and that as strictly and sternly as I could. The truth is, Andreas, that I was angry, so angry that I fairly sparked. When I came in, I felt an almost irresistible urge to go over and give that old man a punch in the nose. I felt he had earned it. When I found a Bible text I thought I could use, I asked the parents if the child had been baptized. "Yes," said the mother. "No," answered the father. Then a cold chill ran down my spine. I felt sick. How these two people could sit there with the dead child between them, and one of them lie, was more than I could comprehend.

I didn't have a great deal of time to reflect, for people had now begun to gather, and many came. During the hymn, I couldn't keep my eyes away from that mother's face. She literally grieved as one who has no hope. Such inexpressible pain and misery I pray God I may never see again. What took place in my soul during the singing, I do not know; I am still not clear about that, but when I began to speak I discarded the text I had just found and instead took the well-known words: "God is love, and he that dwelleth in love dwelleth in God, and God in him." Whether or not that was a fitting text for the occasion, I shall leave unsaid, yet I know that I preached as I have never preached before and perhaps will never preach again. Thoughts and words came of themselves. I felt as if I were but an instrument in a higher hand. Who lied about the child's baptism, I do not know. Presumably what the mother said was true. She may have had the child baptized without telling her husband. We can hope so, at least.

The cemetery was eight miles farther away, and I had to go there too. When I finally bid the parents farewell at the graveside, some words from Bjørnson came to me, which I used. "I hope your son has finally become a blessing to you." "We-e-ll," came slowly from Tor Sima. That was all he said to me, not even a dry "thank you" did I get for my efforts. I got home about midnight, after riding fifty-six miles and preaching a whole hour. You can understand that I was tired, especially when you remember that I had been up half the previous night. Yes indeed, you will experience many strange things in America.

This will be the last letter I'll write to you before you leave Norway, and therefore it becomes my farewell to the Fatherland. Ah well, let's not go into that any deeper, or we'll become sentimental. But before you leave there is one thing I want you to do for me. You must go to the cemetery, to Mother's grave, and bid her farewell from me. You know, sometimes I feel that it isn't right for all of us to leave that lonely grave over there. Still there is nothing to do about it. But you must go there and say good-bye for both of us, Andreas. And when you see the coast of Norway sink into the sea, then you must whisper a farewell from me too. I don't suppose I will ever do it myself.

Now I have no more to say except, "Until we meet in Clarkfield!"

Your loving son and brother,
P. A. Smevik